LOVESWEPT® • 497

Suzanne Forster
Private Dancer

BANTAM BOOKS
NEW YORK • TORONTO • LONDON • SYDNEY • AUCKLAND

PRIVATE DANCER

A Bantam Book / September 1991

If you would be interested in receiving protective vinyl
covers for your Loveswept books, please write to this address
for information:

Loveswept
Bantam Books
P.O. Box 985
Hicksville, NY 11802

ISBN 0-553-44115-9

Published simultaneously in the United States and Canada

Bantam Books are published by Bantam Books, a division
of Bantam Doubleday Dell Publishing Group, Inc. Its trademark, consisting of the words "Bantam Books" and the
portrayal of a rooster, is Registered in U.S. Patent and
Trademark Office and in other countries. Marca Registrada.
Bantam Books, 666 Fifth Avenue, New York, New York
10103.

PRINTED IN THE UNITED STATES OF AMERICA

OPM   0 9 8 7 6 5 4 3 2 1

For Leslie Knowles, who must be a wonderful teacher. Thank you for the vivid insights and the gentle advice.

Private Dancer

One

"Ray Bans, a five o'clock shadow, and a black leather jacket." Bev Brewster whispered the words into the silk flower pinned to her lapel, her eyes riveted on the man who'd just entered The Tearoom Pavilion. Then she glanced around the elegant restaurant to see if anyone had noticed her covert action. Luckily, with all the commotion at the reservations desk, nobody was paying any attention to a rather ordinary-looking brunette, even if she was talking into a flower.

The entire restaurant seemed to share Bev's fascination with the customer the maître d' was discreetly trying to waylay. The man looked as if he'd wandered off a remake of *Rebel Without a Cause*. A poolhall roughneck, Bev thought. What was he doing in a place like this?

"I'm sorry, sir, but our dress code requires a jacket." The maître d's agitated voice carried through the hushed room.

"Then we have no problem, do we?" The roughneck indicated his leather jacket with a flip of the lapel, brushed past the maître d', and entered the room. He hesitated long enough to case the place with one quick sweep of his eyes.

Bev found herself taking in every detail of the man's

appearance, from his shoulder-length dark hair and unshaven profile to his street-brawler's build. He was at least six four and an undeniably tough customer. She didn't envy the maître d's predicament.

The roughneck strolled across the room without a backward glance. He had the long, rangy stride of an urban cowboy and a way of carrying himself that said "proceed at your own risk." He also had the kind of dark, smoldering good looks that women left their husbands for. As he walked, his eyes flicked around the restaurant in a quick appraisal that sized up the trendy crowd with barely concealed insolence.

Bev feigned sudden interest in her menu.

It wasn't just that she wanted to avoid being seen, it was the surprising tightness in her neck muscles. She didn't trust herself not to wrinkle her nose, or to do something even more adolescent, if he looked her way. There was something about the man's go-to-hell attitude that rankled.

Or maybe it was his seeming command of a tense situation, she admitted, taking a quick sip of her oolong tea. Given her present state of insecurity, a show of confidence from anyone, including her pet goldfish, felt threatening. Frankly she didn't feel equal to this assignment, or to *any* assignment. She wasn't a bonafide private eye, and if she hadn't insisted on helping out at her father's detective agency after he'd had his heart attack a month earlier, she wouldn't be here now. She'd still be designing and selling mail-order stationery from her small house in the San Fernando Valley.

"Mind if I sit down?"

The harsh whiskey rasp of a male voice sent shivers down Bev's spine. Her jaw went slack and her head snapped up. "I beg your pardon," she said, staring into empty air. An embarrassing second flashed by before she realized the man hadn't been talking to her. He was two tables down, talking to—

Bev snapped to attention. He was talking to Elayne Greenaway, the woman she'd had under surveillance for the past week. Bev barely had time to be grateful that neither of them had heard her before she registered the oddness of the situation. She wasn't surprised that Mrs. Greenaway was meeting a man. She'd been hired because *Mr.* Greenaway thought his wife was having an affair. What surprised Bev was her subject's choice of man. What could a sophisticated woman like Elayne Greenaway possibly want with a hoodlum like him?

Unless it was the obvious, Bev thought, experiencing a tiny, involuntary shudder. Reckless thrills. Some women went in for that sort of thing, especially bored housewives with money to burn.

No, it had to be a mistake, she decided, expecting to see security guards burst into the room at any moment and drag the intruder away. Instead, she watched him pull back a chair and sit down at Mrs. Greenaway's table as though he'd been invited. A moment later he slouched back negligently, a booted foot propped on his knee.

Bev lowered her menu, fascinated. This was going to be interesting, she decided. The fashionable Mrs. Greenaway hadn't uttered a word of protest. In fact, she was smiling one of those dippy smiles that women often produce when they come flat up against a wall of male sensuality. And he had it to spare, Bev admitted. A six-feet-four-inch wall of it.

A waiter approached hesitantly and the roughneck ordered a beer. The waiter reappeared almost instantly, apparently eager not to offend, but when he tried to pour the beer into a chilled glass, the man stopped him.

He drinks from the bottle, Bev thought, watching him rip off the screw top and take a long swallow. Why didn't that surprise her? He probably chewed on toothpicks and kept a pack of Camels in his rolled-up T-shirt sleeve. He probably didn't even shut the bathroom door!

Bev understood that the first priority of good detective work was emotional distance, but she decided to indulge herself this once. She was already nurturing a dislike for Elayne Greenaway's hoodlum boyfriend, just on principle. He was too cocky and self-assured for his own good—or so she told herself several times over the next few minutes. And then, when she saw him chugalug the first beer and order a second, she made up her mind that he drank too much and probably treated women abominably.

And yet, when Elayne Greenaway leaned across the table and touched his hand, Bev's breath caught. It happened so suddenly she felt a wave of lightheadedness. Elayne's crimson fingernails mesmerized Bev as they drifted lightly across the man's forefinger. Even more bizarre was how Bev could almost imagine herself doing the same thing! For a split second, she envisioned herself in Elayne Greenaway's place. Touching him.

The roughneck glanced down at Elayne's hand, then raised his eyes to hers. It was a scene right out of a sizzling midnight movie, Bev realized, one with Bogart and Bacall. She didn't dare blink for fear of missing something. Riveted in place, she watched as Elayne took a slender cigarette from a gold case and waited for him to light it. He dug a tattered book of matches from a zipper pocket of his jacket and leaned forward, staring into her eyes as he slowly struck the match.

Bev nearly slithered off the chair as he touched Elayne's hand to steady it. It was over in an instant, just the lightest contact of his fingertips against Elayne Greenaway's wrist, but to Bev it ranked sky-high on her list of ecstatic moments. In all her twenty-seven years, she'd never seen anything so sexy!

They began to talk then, in hushed, conspiratorial tones. Bev found herself leaning toward them instinctively, so engrossed that she nearly toppled out of the chair when the roughneck suddenly stood up. He nodded at Mrs. Greenaway. She smiled back at him, and then he turned and walked away.

Bev barely had her pulse rate under control before he'd disappeared from the room. She sat there, oddly shaken, and wondering what to do. Who was he to Mrs. Greenaway? And what had their brief meeting been all about? She'd been following the woman for days and this was the first indication that there might be something clandestine in her life.

Abruptly Bev's instincts took over. *Check it out*, she told herself. *See where he's going!*

She had no idea how much oolong tea cost, but she plunked down a ten-dollar bill and made tracks for the exit. The roughneck was getting into a vintage red Mustang convertible as Bev came out of the restaurant. He obviously hadn't used the valet parking service either. He was parked down the street, just two cars away from her Buick Skylark.

He gunned the Mustang's engine and pulled back, tires screeching, then wheeled out into traffic like a destruction derby veteran. Irresponsible, too, Bev thought, ringing up another character defect. She had quite a list by now.

As he sped down the street, Bev sprinted for her car. Her heart was pounding wildly. She was halfway across the street before she realized that she was actually going after him! She wasn't sure when she'd made that decision, and she suspected her reasons weren't entirely professional, but she simply had to find out who Mrs. Greenaway's hoodlum boyfriend was.

Had she put the blackjack in her purse?

It was the foremost question in Bev's mind as she followed the Mustang through neighborhoods that got progressively seedier. The graffiti grew more explicit by the mile, and the tattooed riffraff loitering on street corners looked as if they were planning their next convenience store heist. Parole violators at best, Bev decided.

Beyond that, Elayne Greenaway's roughneck wasn't an easy man to tail. He drove as if he'd been put on earth to test everyone else's defensive driving skills, including Bev's. She'd nearly lost him twice, and suddenly that didn't seem like such a bad idea. She was just about to make an illegal U-turn and head back when he pulled the Mustang over.

He parked in front of a rundown beer joint called The Red Monkey. The bar was housed in a two-story building with a sign in the window that advertised rooms to rent upstairs. Bev pulled over half a block down the street and waited, sizing up the situation. It was possible this was where he and Elayne Greenaway met, although she couldn't imagine the attorney's wife stepping foot in such a place. Unless Mrs. Greenaway was a closet thrillseeker, she reminded herself, the sort who sought out danger to relieve the tedium of her privileged life.

Twenty minutes later, Bev had accepted the fact that, tedious life or not, Mrs. Greenaway wasn't going to show up. Still burning with curiosity, she told herself she'd come too far not to follow through. She removed her blazer, taking care not to jostle the silk flower. Its petals concealed a tiny microphone attached to a miniature voice-activated tape recorder that Bev had hidden in the breast pocket of her jacket. It was her own brainchild, and she was quite proud of it.

The collar of her linen blouse was lace-trimmed, but Bev flipped it up anyway and freed a couple of buttons. A quick glance in the rearview mirror told her it wasn't enough. With a mother-of-pearl headband restraining her shoulder-length brunette hair, and her unembellished gray eyes, she still looked like the Bev Brewster who shopped at the neighborhood supermarket on Saturday afternoons and recycled aluminum cans.

What bothered her more—far more—was that there were still traces of the Bev Brewster whose husband had left her two years ago for another woman, one who was younger and more fertile. She yanked the headband from her hair and shook her head hard.

Bev entered the bar cautiously and stayed just inside the door, searching the gloom for the roughneck. The Red Monkey was dark, noisy, and crowded, exactly the sort of dive where mayhem loved company and felonies were committed in the alley while no one noticed or cared.

Bev's rapid pulse told her what she already knew, that she was out of her depth. She'd been expecting a den of iniquity, but this was a den of thieves. A concealed-weapons crowd. Even the women loitering at the bar looked like the sort who lured men to the rooms up-stairs and then had their boyfriends roll them.

The roughneck was nowhere in sight. Caution wres-tled with curiosity and won by a landslide. The only thing that kept Bev in place was her own personal demon. She'd had her share of things to feel like a failure about in recent years, and she was determined not to do a repeat with the present situation. She'd gone to great lengths to reassure her father that she could handle a routine surveillance case like this one; the last thing she was going to do was to turn tail and run.

"You're not very good at this, are you?" he said.

A cold chill shimmied down Bev's spine. The sensa-tion was familiar and so was the voice. She'd heard husky undercurrents before, but this guy's voice could crawl up your arm and tap you on the shoulder. She turned and saw him leaning against a wooden post, not five feet away. "Not very good at what?" she asked.

"At following people."

He strolled over to her, and his nearness forced Bev to admit something she'd been trying to ignore in her earlier preoccupation with his defects. He was a highly attractive hoodlum. Even dark glasses and a heavy five o'clock shadow couldn't conceal the strong, slightly asymmetrical bones of his face. His right side was more angular, had more depth, and the effect was strangely sensual. Even his mouth conveyed sensuality. Then Bev noticed the scar that hooked down from the fullness of his lower lip and snaked along his jawline. Had he been knifed? she wondered. Or shot?

"That is what you're doing, isn't it?" he said. She guessed that behind his Ray Bans his gaze was drifting to her unbuttoned neckline. "Following me?"

Bev cocked her head and boldly returned his stare. He had the oddest effect on her. Her heart was racing, her common sense was shouting at her to back off, and yet there she was, sizing him up as though she faced down men in black leather jackets every day.

"My, aren't we vain?" she responded, pleased at the ice-cold tone of her voice. "A woman walks into a bar, and you assume she's following you. Some of us might have better things to do. Or didn't that occur to you?"

"Better things?"

"Yes, as it so happens, I'm meeting someone here— later. I come here often."

"A regular?"

She wondered if his eyes were making a leisurely pass over her body as he mulled over that possibility. Her nerves began to prickle with heat.

"There are two kinds of women who frequent this place," he said, hooking a thumb in a zippered pocket of his jacket, "serious drinkers and private dancers." His smile was as dry as the sawdust on the bar floor. "Which are you?"

There was no doubt what he meant by the latter reference. Bev had already had a look at the female patrons. She might have bluffed about the drinking, except that she had no tolerance whatsoever for alcohol. Two glasses of wine with dinner and she was on her ear. What would Harve Brewster's daughter do now? she thought.

"I dance . . . a little," she finally said, wondering at her less-than-confident tone. The ice in her voice was melting.

His smile turned raffish. "Can I afford you?"

"I doubt it."

He liked that. She could tell by the way he snapped back his head, flicking dark hair off his face. His sunglasses glowed, picking up the neon lights from the bar's beer signs. "I'll take up a collection," he said. Then, pointing out the warped wooden dance floor with a silent jukebox to one side, he added, "Let's do it."

She turned to look, unaware that he was checking her out. He knew she would have blushed if she could have heard his two-word summation of her backside.

Nice butt, he allowed, his eyes following the tailored lines of her slacks as they curved over her hips. Her legs weren't half bad either. Made a man wonder if she knew how to use them. She didn't look as though she'd had a whole lot of practice, he concluded, easing back to survey the whole woman. In fact, if he had to tell the truth, she wasn't his type. He didn't go for fresh-scrubbed complexions and lace collars on grown women. He had noticed her eyes, though, even in the bar's gloom. They were dove gray and soft enough to crawl into. *Soft enough to ease a man's pain*, he thought.

A muscle flexed in his jaw as he let his eyes drift back over her. She might even be a knockout with the right clothes, some makeup, or whatever it was that women did to turn themselves into babes. But who the hell was she?

In the restaurant he'd had her figured for a bored housewife, but bored housewives didn't follow men for ten miles to a bar in one of the roughest parts of town. No, she hadn't come to The Red Monkey for an afternoon of unbridled passion. The moment's regret he felt at that realization didn't make him any less determined to find out what her real motives were. In his business it was dangerous to take anyone for granted, even Ivory soap types with lace collars.

"What's your name?" he asked.

She turned back to him and his breathing held for a split second. The liquid softness of her gaze hit him again, as though it reflected something soft in him, some need. He rejected the idea as insane. There *wasn't* anything soft in him. Not anymore. And as for needs, they got a guy burned. A woman had taught him that.

"Do private dancers have to have names?" she asked.

The anger flickering inside him had little if anything to do with her. It was old business, but its heat had aroused him nonetheless. He couldn't tell if her voice had gone raspy from fear or excitement, but it was clear she intended to play out the game. He resisted the desire to shake his head and laugh. She wasn't a pro, not unless the church-lady look was selling on the streets these days. Whoever she was, it shouldn't take much to call her bluff, especially since he'd been playing this kind of game all his life.

"You're right," he said. "It's better without names."

Say when, lady, he thought, reaching out and capturing a dark tendril of her hair, testing its silkiness with his fingers.

Bev went very still as his skin brushed the delicate flesh just behind her ear. A moment later he was drawing those same fingers along the curve of her throat as lightly as he'd touched Elayne Greenaway.

She was afraid to move as his hand descended, afraid that any sudden gesture would unlock the anticipation trembling inside her. What was he going to do? Actually, she had a fairly good idea, but she hoped fervently that she was wrong. It would be easy enough to stop him, but she knew this was a test of her mettle.

Her heart leaped at the intimacy of his touch, but she willed herself to stay still, unflinchingly still . . . even as his fingers drifted over the rise of her collarbone and down toward the opening of her blouse.

He hesitated a moment, just at the top of her breast, where the skin was exquisitely sensitive. She sensed he was giving her a chance to call it off, but she couldn't bring herself to do it. Her pride was involved. The game had turned into a battle of wills, and she needed to win. If anyone stopped, it would have to be him.

A gasp burned in her throat as he dipped lower, into the warmth between her breasts, into her cleavage. You bastard, she thought. This was outrageous! Her heart raced wildly, and her breasts strained against her bra. And yet she didn't move a muscle. Or try to stop him.

"What do you think you're doing?" she said, barely getting the words out.

She could feel the heat of his stare even through his dark glasses. His nostrils flared slightly as he slipped his hand inside her blouse and cupped her breast.

"This," he said. "How do you like it?"

Her skin flamed with shock and embarrassment. How did she *like* it? She wanted to break every one of his miserable fingers! She averted her eyes, unwilling to let him see her rising fury. He wanted her to react to him. If she moved or even blinked, he would win.

He wasn't going to win, by God! She was. That had become her mission in the past ten seconds. No man was going to make her feel like a whimpering failure again. ·

Her concentration was so intensely focused on his hand that she could feel him searing her flesh through the silk of her bra. Her nipples became painfully engorged, her skin hypersensitive. She could feel every detail of his hand, the roughened texture of his palm, the heartbeat in his fingertips. It was throbbing everywhere, in her breasts, in her throat, in the uncontrollable quiver of her lower lip.

He ran his thumb over the tautness of her nipple. "For a private dancer," he said softly, "you're quick to arouse."

Excitement clenched painfully in Bev's stomach and streamed down her thighs, weakening her legs until she could hardly stand. Her whole body was a quivering mass of nerves. Look at what he was doing to her! Damn him to hell, she thought, anger flaring. She ought to bring up her knee and make a choirboy out of him.

The emotions colliding inside Bev made her act on a dangerous impulse. She didn't bring up her knee, but she did do something that matched him move for move. She lifted the hand that was frozen at her side and placed it squarely on the button fly of his jeans.

His breath caught, and the sound gave Bev intense

satisfaction. She pressed harder, and a thrill rolled up her arm that was as hot as hellfire.

"You're pretty quick to arouse yourself," she said.

He hissed one raw word through his teeth and grimaced in disbelief. "Wh-what the hell are you doing?"

Her fingers curved over the shape of him. "This," she answered. Her heart pounded like crazy as she stared him straight in the Ray Bans. "How do *you* like it?"

"Lady, if you don't get your hand off my pants, you're going to find out how much I like it in about ten seconds."

He wasn't bluffing. All hell was breaking loose beneath the brass buttons of his jeans. But even if he'd been built like a bull elephant and buck naked, Bev wouldn't have removed her hand at that moment.

"Lady, hands off!"

"I will if you will," she countered breathlessly.

The released each other simultaneously and stepped back.

Bev was panting like a winded sprinter. He was breathing hard too, but he had a faint smile on his face that was as intrigued as it was bemused.

"Let's dance," he ordered under his breath.

"No thanks."

He gripped her arm firmly and drew her with him onto the dance floor. "That wasn't an invitation," he said, stopping just long enough to pump some quarters into the jukebox before he took her into his arms. "I don't want the whole damn bar to see the condition I'm in."

Bev wanted nothing more to do with his condition, but she was as limp as a newborn kitten at that moment, and much too weak to object. She was exhausted just thinking about the way she'd groped a man she didn't know.

The music started, a country-western song about cheatin' husbands and cheatin' hearts, and Bev fully expected to be dragged into a hammerlock of an embrace and to be plastered up against his body. He'd given her no reason to think he wasn't the kind of man who danced with his hands all over a woman.

Instead, he held her at a respectable distance, just close enough for camouflage. At first Bev was more confused than relieved. Adrenaline was still coursing through her, and her imagination was conjuring up enough steamy images for an adult video. She was wildly overstimulated, and prepared for just about anything but a display of good manners.

They weren't really dancing, just swaying slowly in time to the music, and she found herself wanting to look up at him, to search his scarred, darkly handsome face and ask him a million questions. Why was a man who terrorized headwaiters, a man who groped strange women and behaved as if life's rules had been written for him to break, suddenly treating her as though this were their first date?

She didn't ask the questions, however. She didn't even look at him. Her head was still swimming with excitement, and she was afraid of what he might see in her eyes.

"I'm curious," he said, his voice made even huskier by the faintest suggestion of masculine laughter. "Do you like it? Dancing, I mean."

She started to nod, then realized he meant *private* dancing. "That depends . . ."

"On what?"

"Oh who I'm dancing with."

She heard his slow intake of air and wondered if she had her answer to his change in attitude. Was he still aroused too? And maybe a little shaken by the force of it? The thought sparked a shower of sensations that strained Bev's already overworked nerves.

"I like this song," she commented, unable to clear the telltale throatiness from her voice. The ice had long ago melted into a warm slush on the barroom floor.

"I like dancing to this song," he said. "With you."

His leg brushed hers and the accidental contact sent a shock wave of expectation through Bev's entire body.

Suddenly she was aware of his hand at the slope of her spine, of its heat and subtle guiding pressure. Her senses heightened with every brush of their bodies. She inhaled deeply, trying to clear her head, and breathed in his scent, rich with aged leather and the tangy, yeasty fragrance of beer.

There was an undeniable thrill in being close to such a man, even if she was loathe to admit it. A woman—*his* woman—would never know what to expect.

Bev was also aware of the music that throbbed from the jukebox, romantic and a little sad. She was a sucker for sad love songs. They plucked at her heartstrings and forced her to acknowledge the sweetness that was missing from her life. The ordeal of her five-year marriage had eroded her confidence and chipped away at her sense of identity, until sometimes she wondered if she would ever feel like a whole woman again.

And yet now, with the melancholy ballad swirling around them, Bev could feel the faint yearnings of womanhood stirring. She'd almost forgotten what it was like to be in a man's arms. It surprised her that the need to be close, to be touched by a man, was still there, still strong. She certainly didn't want to be manhandled again, but for some crazy reason she did want to be held. She wanted to feel a man's strength and sheltering warmth. Just for a moment.

She squeezed his hand without realizing she was doing it.

The answering pressure she felt startled her.

Their dancing slowed to a stop, although Bev's heart began to race. He held her without moving, as though he were waiting for something. "Why won't you look at me?" he asked.

Bev looked up instantly, knowing that any hesitation would put her at a disadvantage. She saw her own reflection in his dark glasses and felt hopelessly exposed. Could he see the fear lurking in her eyes? Could he see the fascination? Did he know that she was hypnotically drawn to what he represented? Thrills. *Reckless thrills.*

He knew. He could see it all, the fear, the erotic flashes of excitement. She was a woman primed for a night of dangerous love. She wanted that lacy blouse taken off her, even if she didn't know it herself. He wasn't sure what attracted him more, her obvious inexperience, or her need to disprove it. But he *was* attracted. Then again, maybe it was her eyes that had him hooked. A man could climb into those eyes and never find his way out. *A man could forget he'd sworn off women like her.*

He smiled and curved his hand to her hip, his fingers drifting over the sudden tension in her buttock. "I don't know who you are," he said, "or why you're here, but I want to dance with you again. Now, *privately.*"

Two

"Privately?" Bev said. "I guess you mean—"

He nodded slowly.

There was no doubt what he meant. So why was she nodding and smiling weakly when she should have been racking her brain for excuses? She felt as though she'd just hit a wall of sensuality head-on—and she wasn't handling the collision any better than Elayne Greenaway had.

Now she understood what Mrs. Greenaway wanted with him. He was the kind of man who made a woman drunk with expectation. Erotic expectation. Everything about him, the leather jacket, the Ray Bans, even the scar that rode his jaw, spoke of smoldering encounters in the dark. Sexually speaking, he was a trapeze act without a net, far too great a risk for the Bev Brewsters of the world.

"Upstairs," he said softly. "You and me, Lace."

"Lace?"

He flicked the lacework on the collar of her blouse. All pretense of social dancing vanished as he encircled her waist and drew her against him, letting his hands glide toward her fanny. Bev gasped as she came into contact with his jeans again. Time had not improved his condition.

"Can I have a raincheck?" she said.

He stared into her eyes, a hot, penetrating stare. Or at least that was what she imagined. His glasses concealed everything but her own anxious expression.

"I have another appointment this afternoon," she explained hastily. "How about later tonight? Nine o'clock?"

"Hold it. Let me get this straight. You want to meet me here later? At nine?"

"Yes . . . that's a wonderful idea," she said as though he'd thought of it. "I could block out an entire hour. Or two, if you'd like more."

"I'd not only like more"—his hands urged her closer, until she could feel every solid inch of the bulge he was trying to hide—"I'd like it *now*."

Panic danced in the pit of Bev's stomach. She had no chance against him physically, and there was no use calling for help. The hooligans hanging around were more disreputable than he was. Bev could see only one way out of the situation—give him what he wanted.

"Right now?" She pulled free of him to check her watch. "Very well." The quick smile she produced said it was all in a day's work, simply a matter of scheduling. "I've got seventeen and a half minutes. Will that be enough time?"

He frowned, the picture of wounded machismo. He was a man who'd just been grievously underestimated. "Seventeen minutes? I'd just be getting started."

It was the reaction Bev had been counting on. She nodded sympathetically. "Oh, of course, how silly of me. Then why don't we meet at nine, as I suggested? We'll have plenty of time, all night if you want."

He gazed down at her a moment longer, and then released her, a sexy grin surfacing. "You're good."

Bev felt another tug of excitement, which she assiduously ignored. She wasn't quite sure what he meant, but she wasn't crazy enough to start asking questions. She was free, and she was leaving.

"Nine, then?" With a breezy nod she backed off the

dance floor, feeling a flash of regret as she turned away from his rampantly sensual smile and his glowing sunglasses. She consoled herself with the fact that she would never forget him standing there in all his rough-neck glory, his arms folded, his hip cocked as he watched her make her escape.

By the time Bev reached her car, she was smiling too, and not only because she'd pulled off a brilliant getaway. Was it possible that the very ordinary Bev Brewster, recycling queen of the Valley, had actually had a sexy brute of a man eating out of her hand! In her mind he wasn't Elayne Greenaway's roughneck anymore, he was hers.

She pulled out into traffic, oblivious to the honks and threats of a passing cabbie. She was too jubilant to worry about defensive driving, or even to let herself dwell on the obvious: that he had let her go without even an argument. That it had all been far too easy.

Bev hadn't lied about the appointment. She simply hadn't mentioned that it was with her father, Harve Brewster, the private investigator of choice in exclusive Beverly Hills. The family agency, Brewster's, was four generations old. Bev's great-great-grandfather had opened the original one-man office on Wilshire at the turn of the century. It had taken every cent he could scrape together, and from those humble beginnings a tradition of unwavering competence and dependability had been built.

The agency had fallen on hard times recently, but it didn't make Bev any less proud of what the Brewsters had achieved, especially her father. At fifty-seven, Harve hadn't lost any of his uncanny ability to read between the lines of a tough case and to sense even the most minor perturbations in the logical order of things. Unfortunately, Bev hadn't inherited her father's analyt-ical genius, but she was good with people, even Harve admitted that. She had a keen intuition going for her and a promising instinct for discerning hidden motives. A "BS detector," her father called it.

As far back as she could remember, Bev had been fascinated by the intricacies of detective work, but Harve had always been reluctant to let her get involved. He wasn't blind to her abilities, he was simply overprotective. She was his only daughter, and she'd never been able to convince him that she could handle the rigors of the business.

Then, just a year ago, the dominoes had begun to fall. Bev's mother had died after a lingering illness, and even though both Bev and Harve had seen it coming, they were rocked by the loss. More recently, two of Brewster's top investigators had defected to form their own agency. And just a month ago Harve had had his heart attack.

Sadly, it was the heart attack that had forced Harve's hand. He had no choice but to let Bev help out at Brewster's. Either that or lose the agency. Now he was convalescing from a triple bypass, stuck in a hospital bed, and ornery as hell. As Bev sat in his private room, giving him a rundown of the day's events, her triumphant escape from the roughneck began to fade under Harve's merciless scrutiny.

"Interesting," Harve snorted as Bev finished her story. He had just tweaked a long, runaway strand from one of the heavy eyebrows that matched his graying hair, and he was pretending to examine the culprit. "And what did you say this guy's name was?"

"I didn't say . . . actually, I didn't get his name."

"Didn't get his name? What about his license plate number?"

"I didn't get that either." Bev's voice slid into a monotone as she began to realize that she'd fluffed a golden opportunity. She didn't know a damn thing about the roughneck, she admitted to herself, not even his eye color!

"Address, phone number, credit cards?"

"Uh . . . no."

"Well, what *did* you get for your trouble, B.J.? Except a handful?"

Bev blushed hotly. In her excitement she'd told Harve the whole story, detail upon detail. It was a tactical mistake. Her father hadn't disapproved of the way she'd "handled" the roughneck. On the contrary, it had given him a good chuckle—and a chance to poke some holes in her procedure.

"I know where he hangs out," she said defensively. "I can go back, ask questions."

"I don't think you want to do that." Harve gentled his gruff voice a little. "He might take you up on that raincheck. Be a fool if he didn't."

Bev let out a tight sigh. "Okay, I admit it," she said, unable to hide the defeat that softened her voice. "I blew it. Like the horn of Gabriel, I blew it."

She dropped back in her chair, and then mentally kicked herself for being such a pill. It was just that she'd wanted so badly to please him, apparently even more than she realized. In the car on the way over, she'd imagined his pride, his smile of approval as she recounted her trial by fire. Instead, he was telling her that she'd messed up royally, and it hurt.

"Don't worry, kid. You've been in the drawer too long, that's all. Once you've had your nose to the grindstone for a while, you'll sharpen up like a dull knife."

Bev made no attempt to hide her confusion. "What are you saying? That you want me to stay on the case?"

"I'm saying that once you get a couple more surveillance cases under your belt, you'll be up to speed. You're quick on your feet and you've got me for a coach." He favored her with a bearish grin. "Hell, you've probably picked up everything you need to know by listening to me all these years."

Bev could hardly believe what she was hearing. What he was doing sounded too much like a magnanimous, fatherly gesture. She knew how concerned he'd been about her since her divorce. He was always tweaking her about how reclusive she'd become. "You shouldn't be burying yourself in that house, B.J.," he was fond of telling her. "Shelve those notepads of yours and get out once in a while, spark your interest in life again. You remember, *life*? Man-woman stuff."

She was fond of telling him that her interest in man-woman stuff didn't need sparking, it needed emergency road service. She wasn't interested.

"I must be getting old." Harve's gravelly voice drew Bev out of her thoughts. "I can remember my first case like it was yesterday," he said as she glanced up.

His nostalgic smile made her heart tighten. He wasn't old. He was in his prime, too vital a man to be confined to a hospital bed. "Your first case? I'll bet you aced it, right?"

"No, I blew the horn, just like you did." He rested his head on the pillow, sighed heavily, and then tossed her a wink. "I envy you, kid. It's fun, isn't it? Even the screwups."

Bev was beginning to understand why he'd relented, perhaps even why he wanted her involved. It wasn't just for her sake, she realized with relief. In a way, he'd been living vicariously through her since he'd been in the hospital. Working with her allowed him to keep his hand in. Her daily visits and their coaching sessions had kept him feeling involved and needed.

Harve hit a button on his adjustable bed and suddenly he was sitting up straighter. "So," he said, reclaiming his trademark gruffness, "what's your next move?"

"I have an appointment with Mr. Greenaway tomorrow morning." She sat forward, eager for his feedback. "Maybe I'll postpone it until I have something more concrete to tell him."

"No, no." Harve waved away her doubts. "Tell him you're checking out his wife's lunch companion, and you'll get back to him when you know something. It's a breakthrough in the case, Bev. You did good."

Bev's eyes narrowed in surprise. You old son of a gun, she thought. He *was* proud. The sudden welling of emotion she felt made it difficult to smile. And then, in the twinkling of an eye—Harve's eye—she felt a flash of the excitement he'd always told her came with a challenging assignment. "The thrill of the chase," he'd called it. Tomorrow she would be back on the beat, investigating the roughneck, checking out every possible lead. As much as that prospect frightened her, it also drew her in some strange way that she didn't want to analyze too closely.

Maybe Harve was right. Maybe this *was* fun?

Someone was following her. Bev hesitated on the fifth-floor landing of the office building's interior stairwell, listening as whoever was on the landing above her stopped too. Solid concrete obscured her vision completely, but she suspected the tail was a man. A metallic click that sounded like a boot heel had alerted her.

She'd come out of Nate Greenaway's office moments before, preoccupied by the brief but difficult meeting. Greenaway had been shaken by the news of his wife's rendezvous, and Bev had felt both sympathy and empathy. Unfortunately, she could neither console nor reassure him that everything would be all right. He'd hired her to be the bearer of his bad news. That was her job.

And now she had someone on her tail. . . .

A good detective's bag of tricks included several ways to lose a shadow, but Bev wanted to learn the person's identity without endangering herself. Her palms were damp, her throat dry, but she was more curious than frightened. Perhaps she had inherited some of her father's coolheaded instincts.

The ground floor exit had a door that squeaked, which Bev hoped would work to her advantage. Whoever opened it behind her would be unknowingly announcing himself. She let the bolt shut quietly, then took cover in an adjacent breezeway to wait and watch.

Seconds flashed by—and became minutes. Bev kept her eye on the door as she weighed the possibilities. Her pursuer might have used another exit. Or perhaps she hadn't been followed after all. She'd simply heard someone who worked in the building descending to a lower floor.

She decided to check it out. Slipping a hand into her shoulder bag, she gripped the blackjack lightly and crept along the wall toward the door. The staccato click of a typewriter drifted from an open window, but Bev barely registered the sound. She was totally focused on the door. And who might be behind it.

She reached her destination and hesitated a moment, listening. The knob twisted noiselessly in her damp palm as she turned it. She let the door creak open, then give it a quick, hard shove. The stairway pulsed with an unseen presence.

Bev's fingers tightened around the weapon in her bag as she scanned the emptiness. Every survival instinct she had told her to back off, to get out of there. But something wouldn't let her run. Her pride was involved. She had no intention of reporting another screwup to Harve.

She opened the door wider with her foot.

A hand flashed out of nowhere, so suddenly she couldn't scream. It snagged her by the wrist and dragged her into the stairwell. "Stop!" she cried, yanking the blackjack from her bag. She swung at her assailant, catching the shadowy form somewhere on the head.

There was a sharp crack, a muffled grunt of pain, and the man slumped to the cement floor at her feet. Bev reared back, a scream locked in her throat. She gaped at the sprawled body. He was lying facedown and the lights were too dim to see what kind of damage she'd done, but fear and revulsion ran riot in her mind, spiking her imagination. Was he alive?

Her brain was spinning so fast she couldn't think what to do. Call an ambulance? The police? He was as still as death itself, and his upper torso was twisted oddly, which told her he probably wasn't faking unconsciousness. She waited several more seconds, and when he didn't move, she approached cautiously, nudging him with her foot. His body was limp and unresponsive.

She dropped to her knees and struggled to roll him over, aware that there was something familiar about him. He was wearing dark glasses! It was impossible to make out his features in the gloom, but Bev had a terrible feeling she knew who he was. Once she had him on his back, she threw open the exit door.

Light flooded in, revealing an angular jawline and a scar that snaked out from his chin. It *was* him, the roughneck. A pool of blood had collected on the cement floor, and the sight of it gave her a rush of queasiness.

She forced herself to press her fingers to a carotid artery in his neck, praying for a pulse. She found one, and it was strong. He wasn't dead; he was very much alive.

She left out the taut breath she'd been holding. Her dad had assured her that she was a quick study, but he hadn't warned her that the past two days would be a crash course in cloak and dagger work. Maybe in theory this was fun, but in practice it felt more gruesome.

She deliberated, knowing she ought to call an ambulance immediately. If the situation hadn't presented her with such a perfect opportunity to find out who he was, she probably would have. But instead, her investigative instincts took over.

It took some twisting and pulling on her part, but she found his wallet in the left back pocket of his jeans. Either he was a lefty, or he was trying to throw off pickpockets. A quick inspection revealed an assortment of business and ID cards, each with a different name. She still didn't know who he was. A con man? Or a private eye, like herself? Both relied on false identities. Lost in concentration, she bent over him to return the wallet.

"Oh!" she cried as a hand manacled her wrist. She reared back instinctively, the sudden shock throwing her off balance. She was already toppling as he pulled her over his body and rolled her onto her back on the cement floor.

"What are you doing?" She got the words out seconds before he swung himself on top of her and clamped a hand to her mouth.

He glared down at her, his dark hair matted with blood, his jaw contorted with pain. "Let's put it this way," he said, grinding out the words with considerable effort. "I'm not asking you to dance."

She twisted free of the hand that muzzled her. "Let go of me!"

"Not a chance, babe. Knocking a guy unconscious and going for his wallet isn't the way to win friends and influence people. Or hasn't anybody told you that?" He caught hold of both her hands, subduing her struggles with infuriating ease. His grip was iron. The muscles that layered his forearms and the straining cords that braced his neck were evident even in the dim light.

Panic ripped through Bev as she realized how helpless she was. She was pinned to the cement floor by his weight, unable to move. Even her breathing was constricted. She searched his face, frantic for clues, for anything that would help her predict what he might do next. He may have been knocked unconscious, but he wasn't nearly as badly hurt as she'd thought. In her panic she'd forgotten that even a minor head wound could bleed like crazy.

His clenched jaw told her he was fighting the pain of his injury. She prayed that would keep him occupied for a while, and yet the grim smile that formed as he stared down at her was as sensual as anything Bev had ever seen. He was aware of the paralyzing intimacy of their situation. His eyes flickered with dark impulses. It wasn't murder she saw in their depths, but something almost as frightening under the circumstances. She saw raw glints of sexuality, the undeniable heat of male interest.

"Let me go," she said again.

"Sure thing, Lace." His gaze dropped to her mouth,

to her trembling lower lip, and his voice went husky. "Just as soon as I'm done with you."

"What does that mean?" Did this have something to do with the private dancer thing? Had he tracked her down because of yesterday? Fear made her voice raspy. "Have you been tailing me?"

"Watch how you talk," he said, laughing as he pinned her hands to the floor on either side of her head. "You'll give me ideas." The movement brought his face perilously close to hers so that Bev caught the rich tang of coffee on his breath. He shifted over her, and she felt the powerful muscles of his inner thighs.

Her stomach muscles pulled tight. There was a hot sparkle of sensation somewhere deep inside her that she refused to acknowledge as anything but fear. "I think you should let me up," she said. "This instant."

"I think you should keep your appointments," he answered back. "Let's see. Where did we leave off in the bar?"

Bev remembered exactly where they'd left off in the bar—with her pressed up against his jeans and frantically negotiating her way out of a session upstairs. As for him, he'd been as ready to go as a stud Thoroughbred. "No, you can't—"

"Sure, I can. I'm on top."

"No! I mean not like this! That would be . . ."

"What? Taking you against your will? Rape?" His eyes flared with an emotion that might have been anger. "Now, there's a thought. She lies to me. She stands me up, knocks me cold, and tries to pick my pocket. And then, as if that weren't enough, she accuses me of sexual assault. No thanks. I like my women willing."

Bev sighed, limp with relief. "Thank God for that."

"Don't thank Him too quickly." He sat back on his haunches, keeping her wrists locked in an iron grip, and checked her out. A smile stole into his expression as he took in her quick, deep breaths, her disheveled hair. "You've got the look of a willing woman to me," he told her. "Your face is warm and flushed, your eyes are dilated. In fact, you're . . ."

She glanced up at him suspiciously. "What?"

"Damn near beautiful," he said after a moment of thought. "How did I miss that yesterday?"

Bev's heart was pounding. Why had he said that? He didn't seem to be the kind of man who paid compliments lightly, if at all. He actually thought she was beautiful? "Leave my looks out of this," she insisted weakly. "And as for that willing-woman business—not a chance. Never."

"Never's a risky word. It makes a man want to prove you wrong." He stared straight into her eyes, daring her not to respond as he drew his fingers down her throat. Bev could feel a trail of hot sparks as he traced the arc of her collarbone and dipped lower into the warmth of her cleavage.

"Don't you dare touch me there!" she warned.

"You sure about that?" he said, his fingers nestling against her trembling flesh. "I had the feeling you loved having your breasts handled. You nearly purred when I did it yesterday."

Purr? Bev Brewster *purr*? Had he been dropped as a child? He was either crazy or too damn egotistical! She let out a gasp as he slipped his fingers inside her blouse. The sudden shock of his skin against her breasts made her moan aloud.

"See there," he said softly. "You do like it."

Bev flushed from the roots of her sable hair, but it wasn't from excitement, it was from anger. She wrenched a hand free, drew it back, and caught him alongside the jaw with a stunning blow.

He stared at her a moment, dazed, and then shook his head as though he could hear something rattling inside. Bev watched him, breath held. Under other circumstances the blow probably wouldn't have fazed him, but he had already been knocked unconscious once. He also had a nasty head wound, and it was possible he'd been in shock all along. At that moment he didn't seem to have any idea what had hit him, and Bev wasn't about to oblige him with an explanation. He was squinting at her as though she were an out-of-focus television set.

"Get off me!" she cried. She thrashed and twisted, desperate to dislodge him.

"I love it when a woman gets rough," he said, leaning back.

Bev had him on the ropes and she had no intention of letting him get away. "Then you should love this." She pushed him with all her might. He was a massive, seemingly immovable object, but she could feel him beginning to give way. As he started to sway, she slid out from under him, escaping just in time to see him topple to the floor.

At first she thought he was unconscious again, but he rolled to his back and opened one eye, grimacing with pain. "What did you hit me with?" he said, touching his jaw. The head wound had opened up again and blood was flowing freely.

"I'm calling an ambulance," Bev said.

"No," he rasped, waving her off. "No doctors. I'll be all right." He dragged himself to the stairway and propped himself against the bottom step, squinting at her as though he were trying to focus. "Just get me to my place, okay?"

"Your place? Where is that?"

"El Monte."

"El Monte? You're half dead and that's three freeways from here. We'll hit traffic. It'll take hours."

"An hour and a half," he said, wincing as he probed the injury with his fingers. "I'll make it. It's a bad cut, that's all, a slight contusion." He flashed her an accusatory glare. "It's my jaw that hurts."

He sounded pretty sure of his condition, but Bev wasn't about to get caught in an L.A. traffic jam with a bleeding man in her car. Getting him to a hospital without his cooperation wasn't going to be easy though. As she tried to decide what to do, she noticed a scrap of paper on the floor. She bent and swept it up, careful to stay out of his range. The top item jumped out at her first. It was the license plate number of her own car! Below it were her address and her phone number.

Her hand began to tremble and her head snapped up. "Who are you?" she said, drilling him with her eyes. "And what do you want with me?"

Three

He didn't answer, and Bev decided she'd had enough of playing around. Confident that he wasn't going anywhere in his state, she left him to get her car. She pulled up by the stairway, and with considerable effort managed to put him in the passenger seat.

As she drove, she wondered at his silence. He should be demanding to know where she was taking him. Had he fainted again? She snuck a look at him and saw that he was slumped back against the seat, resting his head.

She concentrated on maneuvering down Interstate 5 once more. When she finally heard his whispered question, it was so faint, she almost didn't catch it.

"Where are we going?" he'd asked.

"My place."

"*Your* place?"

Bev could hear the surprise in his voice as she headed toward an exit. "My place," she said firmly. "Unless you'd rather go to a hospital. You could probably use a good tetanus shot."

"There's no such thing as a good tetanus shot."

She glanced at him again and wondered if she'd made the right choice. She wasn't worried about her own safety at this point. She was worried about him. He was as limp as wet tissue, and even if he wouldn't admit it, he probably did need medical attention. She ought to take him to a hospital whether he wanted to go or not, but she'd decided not to. A hospital wasn't the right environment for getting the answers she wanted. He'd gone to a lot of trouble to track her down, and she wanted to know why. She was *burning* to know why.

He rolled his head to look at her. "So why your place?"

"I know the way," she said.

He managed a pained grin that bordered on being boyish. "Can't get enough of me, can you?"

She discouraged him with a stern look. He definitely needed a doctor. He was obviously suffering from brain damage.

By the time she pulled into the driveway of her small Encino home, her passenger was beginning to recover some of his macho vigor. He insisted on getting into the house on his own steam, although she noticed that he sagged onto her sectional couch as soon as he reached it.

She went in search of antiseptic and bandages, wondering what he thought of her spic-and-span two-bedroom home. If he still had any illusions about her being a private dancer, her living room decor should put them to rest. The needlepoint throw pillows and the "Bless This Mess" telephone message corkboard were strictly Donna Reed stuff. She smiled to herself, enjoying the possibility that she might have him slightly confused. She'd always wanted to be a woman of mystery—inexplicable, and therefore irresistible to the opposite sex.

Moments later she sat on the arm of the sofa, bending over him to clean the encrusted blood from his temple. His aviator sunglasses were in the way, and as she carefully removed them, she had the oddest sense that she was invading his privacy. Fortunately he accepted her ministrations without comment. His eyes closed while she worked gently with the damp washcloth. To her relief, his head wound turned out to be nothing more than a small laceration.

Once she had the cut cleaned and bandaged, she smoothed the washcloth over his forehead. He felt warmer than normal, but her thoughts wouldn't focus on his temperature. Instead, they dwelled on the unrelieved bones of his face, the faint lines that spidered out from his eyes and the jagged scar. He had the face of a man who lived on the brink of risk and ruination, she decided. Perhaps even a man who had ventured so deeply into the heart of darkness that he hadn't quite made it back.

As she tried to smooth the cloth over his cheekbones and down toward his jaw, he caught her hand and turned his head to face her, his eyes opening slowly. "What are you doing?"

His eyes gave her a shock. It was the first time she'd seen them, and they were a pale shade of blue. Powder blue, she decided. It was an inconceivable color for a man like him. She couldn't decide whether she liked the effect or not. Then she was startled even more by the flicker of apprehension in their depths. Apprehensive? Him? The man who hung out in honkytonks, probably drank his beer straight from the can and crushed the empties against his head? He was primal and raunchy enough for ten men! And yet she felt an unaccountable welling of tenderness for him. The tough guy with baby-blue eyes, she thought, smiling to herself. Lord, she hoped the emotion didn't show.

His voice turned harsh. "I asked what you were doing."

"You're feverish," she told him. "I thought the cold cloth might feel good."

"I don't need a nurse," he said abruptly, waving her hand away. "I need a drink. And make it booze."

What a crude, insufferably rude—she bit back the angry retort on her lips. She couldn't afford to alienate him now. She had a whole battery of questions to ask, and she wanted him receptive, the ingrate.

"Did it ever occur to you to ask rather than order?" she said quietly, rising to get him the drink. She had every intention of making it a stiff one. Maybe alcohol would loosen his tongue.

She crossed the room to the mahogany sideboard that had been a wedding gift from her ex–in-laws, poured several splashes of brandy into a snifter, returned, and plunked it down in front of him on the coffee table. She then took the wing chair across from him, smiling as she sat down. "Need a coaster?" she inquired, casually opening the drawer of the table next to her chair.

"A what?" he said, grimacing. "No, forget it."

She settled back in the chair. "You're welcome."

He took a long swallow of the brandy, shuddered, hit his chest, and took another. "Good stuff," he said, looking up.

Since it was probably the closest thing she would ever get to a compliment from him, Bev nodded graciously. Either the man had been raised by wolves, or he went out of his way to be obnoxious. Something told her it was the latter, especially as she watched him toss back the rest of the brandy. For one thing, he knew how to hold a snifter.

His comment about the brandy sank in. It ought to be good stuff, she thought. It was one of the gifts she'd given her ex-husband, Paul, in the last months of their five-year marriage. Her reaction to her husband's pulling away from her had been to compensate with lavish amounts of attention and needlessly expensive gifts. It wasn't her style at all, but she was desperate to make up for the things she couldn't give him, the things he really wanted. The thought of another failure had been unendurable at that point in her life, and losing Paul had been the ultimate failure.

You're on thin ice, Bev, she told herself. She quickly pushed the memories of her marriage away, knowing she was on dangerous ground. The real reason she and Paul had split up was far too painful to draw out and examine now. Besides, she had more immediate things to concentrate on, such as taking advantage of her guest's weakened condition.

"You went to a lot of trouble to find me," she said. "Mind telling me how you did it?"

He shrugged and dark hair fell forward, almost tumbling into his eyes. "No trouble at all," he answered, sweeping the hair back. "I had a hunch you were giving me the slip yesterday, so I checked out your license plate number as you were pulling away from the bar."

"And my address? How did you get that?"

"Friends at the DMV."

She asked the next question without missing a beat. "Why were you so eager to find me?"

"You don't know?"

"You just couldn't get enough of me?" She smiled, and then almost wished she hadn't said the words as his baby blues drifted to more intimate areas of her anatomy, including her breasts, which were already overly responsive to his displays of interest.

"Not nearly enough," he said. "Care to remedy that?"

"Maybe . . . when I get some honest answers."

His eyes flashed with the same dark impulses she'd seen when she was pinned beneath him in the stairway landing. Sexual bargaining seemed the only ploy that worked with him, and the awareness sent a strange thrill of excitement through her. Of course, she couldn't consider such a thing again. She'd already had two narrow escapes. It would be utterly crazy . . . and yet she couldn't deny that there was something about him that made her want to take risks. What was it? His moody, gimme-what-I-want-baby good looks? The air of reckless sensuality?

Fortunately, he took the decision out of her hands.

"Rules of the game," he said as he set the snifter down. "The first is don't make promises you don't intend to keep. Sooner or later some tough customer is going to call your bluff."

"But not a nice guy like you."

He grinned, dug a toothpick out of his jacket pocket, and popped it into his mouth. "Right," he answered lazily, letting the toothpick roll to the corner of his lips. "I'm a regular prince."

"Then how about answering my questions, your highness. Like who are you? I mean, who are you really?"

He shook his head slowly. "Rule number two—don't ask questions you don't want answers to."

"But I *do* want answers."

"No, you don't."

Bev swallowed a sigh of frustration. He was as impossible to pin down as a flickering shadow. She tapped her fingers on the table as it gradually dawned on her that she did have a bargaining tool other than her body. A very potent bargaining tool. She slipped her hand into the table's open drawer and pulled out the .45 automatic handgun she kept there. "Oh, yes, I do," she said.

A grimace of disbelief crept into his expression as he stared at her, and the toothpick nearly fell out of his mouth.

Bev quelled a nervous smile. The gun was a model designed to look real even at close range. Her father, who didn't believe in carrying weapons, had given it to her and lectured her thoroughly on its use. He'd warned her it was a good way to get shot if used recklessly, so she doubted he'd approve of her tactics now. But she just couldn't resist turning the tables on Mr. Tough Customer.

"So tell me," she continued, her heart pounding, "who are you anyway? When you're not being a prince."

Bev watched him, trying to predict what he might do next as he pulled the toothpick from his mouth and scrutinized her. She'd thought he might be amused by it all, but he didn't look the least bit amused. His eyes had gone from baby blue to the color of ice, and his darkening mood was all too obvious. He looked as though a hailstorm of biblical proportions was gathering directly above his head. But surely he wouldn't be foolish enough to rush a woman with a gun.

Bev had no idea how much he *wanted* to rush her. He'd already imagined the pleasure of wrestling the gun out of her hand in graphic detail—and then he'd rejected the idea. She obviously wanted some information, and so did he. Maybe they could do some trading. "What do you want to know?" he asked, noting her sigh of relief.

The gun dipped in her hand, and he fought back the desire to take it away from her, just on principle. Physically it would have been a cakewalk. She was no match for a man his size, but she had her act together, he had to admit that. She'd faked him out twice in twenty-four hours, and he couldn't remember the last time that had happened.

Maybe it was those lace collars she wore, or the wistful, worried, who-am-I expression he'd noticed once or twice in her dove-gray eyes. He'd been distracted by women before, plenty of times, but the reason had always been sex. With her, it was sex too, and then more. She had the damnedest way of making him feel as though he ought to be nice to her.

"Who are you?" she asked tentatively, as though she'd been trying to analyze his contemplative mood. "I mean, who are you really?"

He popped the toothpick in his mouth again and sat back, draping an arm across the back of the couch. "Name's Sam Nichols."

A frown formed. "You've got twenty IDs in your wallet," she said, rubbing the gun barrel absently against her thigh. "Not one of them said Sam Nichols."

He decided to make it easy for her. "That's because it's my real name."

"Why all the IDs?"

He grinned, knowing she wouldn't believe him. "I'm a collector."

"A collector? Of business cards? My, what an absorbing hobby." She stood up and strolled across the room, watching him thoughtfully, and swinging the gun as though she'd forgotten all about it. In fact, she was making him damn nervous the way she was handling that weapon.

"So . . . what is it you want with me, Sam?" The gun barrel ticked back and forth like a metronome, and then, as though she'd just remembered it, she began to tap her chin with it, slowly, almost sensually. "My business card?" She cocked her head in a sexy way.

He rolled the toothpick around in his mouth and crunched down on it. Oh, now he really did want to wrestle her to the ground. Hell, she was as unpredictable as a broken compass needle. She was straightlaced one minute, wistful and curious the next—and then there was this sex-bunny-with-a-gun thing.

"I said, what do you want with me, Sam?"

She was rubbing the barrel against her cheek now, almost as though she were about to kiss the damn thing! She hadn't forgotten the gun, she was flaunting it! She'd had a little taste of power and she liked it. That was dangerous when a woman had a .45 in her hand, and if she got any cockier, he was going to take it the hell away from her. He snapped the toothpick between his teeth to keep from smiling. She was kind of cute when she got all fired up.

"Am I going to get an answer? Sam?"

"I was hired to tail you."

"What?"

Sam scores, he thought. Finally. "I'm a private dick— uh, you know, detective. And you're my subject."

She'd been approaching the coffee table as they talked, and it was a good thing there was a chair behind her, or she would have ended up on the floor. "You're kidding me?" she said, sinking into the wing chair.

"Never been more serious. I had Nate Greenaway's office staked out this morning when you walked in."

"Staked out?"

"His wife, Elayne, hired me."

"Mrs. Greenaway hired a private detective?"

He nodded, and she began laughing softly. "This is unbelievable," she said, once more oblivious to the weapon she was waving as she talked. "I'm working for

Mr. Greenaway. He hired me to check up on his wife because he thought she was cheating."

"Could you watch where you're pointing that thing?"

"Oh, sure," she said, dropping the gun onto the table. "You know, it's all starting to make sense now. I took you for Mrs. Greenaway's boyfriend, and that's why I followed you to the bar. You must have thought I was crazy."

"It crossed my mind." Several times, he thought, like a ping-pong ball in tournament play.

She leaned forward, elbows on her knees, gazing at him as though she were looking for tangible proof of what he'd just told her. "Amazing," she said, "I never would have figured you for a private eye."

"Yeah, me too," he said. "I mean, you had me fooled."

She *was* kind of cute, he decided. Her wardrobe left a lot to be desired, and he would never understand why a grown woman wanted to strangle such sexy hair in a band. But she was flushed and excited about something. In fact, she was damn near beautiful at the moment, just like yesterday in the bar.

"Did you think I was Mr. Greenaway's lover?" she asked.

"No, but I was curious what you were doing there. It seemed coincidental, so I decided to check it out."

"Oh." Bev was a little disappointed in his answer. She would like to have been thought of as someone's paramour. And she rather liked the idea that he might have been following her simply because he'd been so totally fascinated with her. Well, at least he'd taken down her license plate number.

"Would you like something cold to drink?" she asked, aware that her throat was exceedingly dry. Nerves, she imagined. A great deal of excitement had been packed into the last two days.

"Sure, got a beer?"

"Iced tea?"

Sam hated iced tea, but he gave her a quick nod just for the opportunity of watching her walk to the kitchen.

As soon as she'd left the room, he picked up the revolver and smiled. Score another point for her, he thought. She *was* good. He set down the bogus weapon and did a quick visual search of the area.

There was no sign of a man in residence, but there were plenty of signs to confirm his first impression of her. The spotless house, the needlepoint and lace doilies put her squarely in the "nice" category. She might have a few quirks—who didn't—but she was a missionary at heart. He'd had enough experience with the type to spot one. Nice women went feverish at the sight of a back-slider like him, only it wasn't sex they wanted. It was reformation. They wanted to get him shaving regularly, combing his hair, and updating his wardrobe. They weren't hot for making babies, they were hot for table manners and good grooming.

Case in point, he told himself as she walked back into the room carrying two tall glasses with lemon wedges stuck on the rims. She already had him drinking iced tea instead of beer. By next week she'd have confiscated his toothpicks.

He'd been through that before. His ex-wife had married him as an act of rebellion against her conservative parents. When the glow wore off and she realized that his pose was for real, that with Sam Nichols what you saw was what you got, she'd bailed out. Just when he'd needed her most.

"By the way, I'm Bev Brewster," she said, handing him the glass rather than setting it on the table. "And we have a problem." Smiling, she took a seat next to him on the sofa. "What are we going to do about our clients?"

"Well, for one thing, we can stop tailing each other," he suggested, edging away from her. "That would save them both some money."

She drank deeply from her glass. "No. I mean, it's obvious the Greenaways don't need private eyes. They need to talk. Neither one of them is cheating, but they're not communicating either. They don't trust each other."

Sam set his iced tea on the table, untouched. "That

may be true, but Mrs. Greenaway isn't paying me for my psychological insights. She's paying me to tail her husband."

"Yes, but only because she believes he's being unfaithful."

Sam could see where the discussion was headed. Any minute now she'd be lecturing him on the ethics of servicing a client who obviously didn't need the service. He wanted to concede her point about as much as he wanted to be hijacked by terrorists, but he knew anything less would get him embroiled in a long-drawn-out, no-win argument.

"So what do you suggest?" he said with barely veiled sarcasm. "That we advise our clients to sit down and have a heart-to-heart?"

"Yes!" Bev jumped on the idea immediately. "That's exactly what they need to do, Sam. If they'd talked in the first place, they wouldn't have had to hire us, would they?" She was surprised and delighted that he'd brought up the idea, even if reluctantly. Maybe he was a reasonable man after all.

"Do you have an office in the city?" she asked, suddenly curious. She gazed at him intently, noticing the length of his lashes and the way his eyelids drooped slightly at the outer corners. Only their arresting pale blue color kept them from being bedroom eyes.

Sam felt like telling her he worked out of his car, but he knew that would only encourage her maternal instincts. "A small office in El Monte. Very small."

Bev barely noticed Sam's mumbled reticence. She wanted to know more about him, especially now that they had their work in common. And she'd been vastly relieved to learn that he wasn't a rapist, or a felon, or any of the other things she'd imagined. "Do you work alone?"

"Strictly alone," he said, glancing at her front door.

Sam was only half listening as Bev pressed on with her questions. He was planning his escape. Maybe he could tell her he was due somewhere, anywhere. He wanted badly to come up with an excuse and cut out before she got to the personal stuff, like his marital status and his yearly income. He knew how missionaries operated. They weren't happy until they'd ferreted every secret a guy had.

The only thing keeping him there was his fascination with her hands. She was doing something a man didn't often see a woman do in polite company. She was playing with his drink.

She'd finished her own long ago, and he'd seen her glance at his several times. At first he'd thought it was because she was still thirsty, but then he realized something else was going on. She leaned forward, absently dipped her finger into the iced tea, twirled it around and brought the finger to her lips. Her face was slightly flushed, and her eyes were sparkling as she talked and laughed, carrying the conversation, but she wasn't being openly seductive. He wondered if she was even aware that she was doing it.

"You really like iced tea, don't you?" he asked softly.

She glanced down at her finger and yanked it out of the liquid as though she'd been scalded. "Oh! I'm so sorry," she said. "I'll get you another glass."

She was off to the kitchen before he could stop her, and suddenly he wasn't in such a big rush to leave. Maybe he'd been too quick to pigeonhole Bev Brewster. A woman who carried a blackjack in her purse and kept a fake revolver in her living room had some instincts that weren't missionarylike at all.

He dug another toothpick out of his pocket and placed it between his lips. As for playing with his drink . . . that was one of the sexiest things he'd ever seen a woman do.

Four

Bev's hands were shaking as she opened the freezer compartment of the refrigerator to get some ice. She filled the glass quickly, her fingertips stinging from the cold. Her face was stinging too, but it was for a different reason. She'd exposed an aspect of herself to Sam Nichols that she was profoundly uncomfortable with. It wasn't just iced tea she liked, as he'd suggested. It was water, liquid, anything wet. She had a . . . well, she didn't know what to call it, but a fetish for wetness.

She'd never gone to a psychiatrist to find out why. She'd been too embarrassed. It had probably stemmed from a silly incident in her childhood. Besides, as annoying as the affliction was, it never became a problem unless she was aroused. And up until forty-eight hours ago, she hadn't been aroused in a long time.

Icy steam roiled out from the freezer compartment as Bev returned to her immediate problem. She hadn't actually put her finger in her mouth, had she? Not right in front of him!

She slammed the freezer door and picked up the pitcher of iced tea on the kitchen counter, filling the glass to the brim. Maybe he hadn't really noticed . . . or read anything into it.

"Bev?"

She turned and saw him standing in the kitchen doorway, leaning negligently against the doorjamb, his expression subtly alert. Her heart sank. He'd noticed, all right. He had the look of a man whose curiosity had been aroused, among other things.

"Is that what you like to be called?" he asked. "Bev?"

"Actually, my father calls me B.J." She had no idea why she'd volunteered the information. She didn't want Sam Nichols calling her that. She didn't even want her father calling her that.

A smile appeared on his lips and almost drifted to his eyes. "B.J. That's a name with possibilities."

"I've got your iced tea," she said, holding out the glass.

"I don't want any more iced tea."

Somehow that didn't surprise her. She clutched the glass in both hands and told herself to put it down. Instead, she watched him push away from the door and stand tall. His head wasn't half a foot from the top of the doorway, she realized. He was that big a man.

"Have you been thinking about it too, B.J.?" A faint huskiness snuck into his voice. "Thinking about it the way I have?"

"Thinking? About what?"

"The way I touched you yesterday. The way you touched me."

She shook her head and turned away from him, setting the glass down on the counter too quickly. Iced tea sloshed over and the lemon wedge tumbled off the rim. Bev breathed in so deeply, the sharp tang of citrus burned her nostrils.

"Why would I be thinking about that?" she said, grabbing a cloth to mop up the spill. She sounded out of breath and hopelessly insincere.

"Maybe because it was exciting."

She heard him come up behind her and sent up a quick prayer for self-control. The other times they'd been together, he'd been shockingly aggressive, and she'd reacted more out of self-defense than arousal.

This was different. He was different. Quiet, smoky-voiced, alive with sexual danger.

"Was it exciting?"

She tossed off an answer that was meant to be noncommittal. "What if it was? Buying a new dress is exciting."

"I don't know what you were shopping for, lady, but it wasn't dresses." He drew closer, his voice a rough caress. "You gave me one hell of a jolt. And don't tell me you didn't know it."

Bev felt the heat coming off his body. It ran the length of her back, accumulating in all those nerve-rich places where she was anticipating contact. Her calves were tingling, her shoulder blades, even her buttocks. He hadn't touched her, but he was driving her crazy wondering when he would.

"Stop it," she said.

"What? I haven't done anything. Except try to answer your question."

"What question?"

"You asked me why you should be thinking about yesterday. Why you should remember what we did and the way it made you feel." He became silent for a moment. "You still haven't answered my question. Did you find it exciting when I touched you?"

She felt something brush against the back of her thigh, and her imagination went off like a rocket. Was it his knee? His hand? She pressed against the counter-top, her hipbones coming into contact with the cold ceramic tile. There wasn't going to be a repeat of yesterday's "excitement." She had no intention of letting him fondle her again.

He let out a low, sexy gust of laughter that lifted the damp hairs on her neck. "I don't think that counter's going anywhere. You can relax your grip on it."

"Stop it," she ordered, whirling around to face him. "I want you to stop it! Now."

"Stop what?"

The question threw her into a quandary. "I don't

know. Whatever it is you're doing." The problem was he wasn't doing anything, at least not anything physical. "You're intimidating me with words," she said, "baiting and teasing, playing with me. I'm not a child, for heaven's sake. I can't be turned on and off like some battery-operated toy."

"Interesting concept." He studied her through low-ered lashes, his expression flickering with curiosity and a blue-eyed arrogance that was distinctly male, dis-tinctly him. "As for the child business," he said, "that was the furthest thing from my mind. You don't look like a child. You don't *feel* like a child. If I'm playing with you, it's an adult game and you qualify."

He raised his hand, a lazy arc of motion. Bev flinched back, certain that he was going to touch her in some way, perhaps even intimately.

"Don't try to kid yourself, Lace, or me," he said, rolling the toothpick between his fingers before he took it from his mouth and flicked it into her kitchen sink. "I'm not calling the shots here. You're woman enough to have a man if you want one, and simply because you want one."

"Stop it," she whispered again. He was so close she couldn't breathe. She looked down, trying to escape the probing blue of his eyes. What she got for her effort was a breathtaking view of a man's lower body, muscular and endlessly rangy. Encased in faded jeans, his thighs made her think of the weapon she carried in her purse—a steely blackjack sheathed in soft leather. And because he was standing with one hip cocked, her eyes darted irresistibly to the front of his jeans, where stress lines fanned out from material pulled too tight.

God, what was she doing cornered in her own kitchen by a man like him? He was sex personified. And why was she letting him talk to her about such private things? Even she and Paul didn't discuss the way they touched each other. Obviously, she hadn't weighed the consequences of bringing Sam Nichols to her house.

"I think it might be a good idea if you left," she said without looking up.

"I think it might be the worst idea I've ever heard."

She felt him touching her hair and realized he was removing her headband. As dark waves tumbled around her face, he eased his hand to her nape, gathered a fistful of locks, and slowly drew her head back, willing her to look up at him.

"Something tells me we're just getting started, Lace."

His voice was soft, but Bev could feel the force behind it. Inexplicably, she didn't fight him. Not because she was startled into submission but because looking up and meeting his eyes had a slow, paralyzing effect on her. There was a natural gauntness in his features that spoke of hunger and dark impulses. He wasn't the kind of man who seduced a woman for hours and hours, she realized. She couldn't imagine him waiting patiently until a woman was ready, or putting a woman's pleasure before his own. There was a roughness in him, a simmering promise of violence. He was a throwback to primitive times when survival depended on raw, brute strength. When Sam Nichols wanted something, he didn't wait to be invited, he took it.

Bev realized all that in the matter of seconds, and with the flood of information came another awareness. She wasn't breathing. Her whole body seemed to be caught in a spasm of expectation, waiting to see what he would do next.

"I want to touch you again," he said. "I want to slip my hand inside your blouse and feel your breath catch."

He freed the top button of her blouse and Bev let out a sound that made him smile.

She clutched at his hand. "That was a gasp! People gasp when they're being physically assaulted. It has nothing to do with arousal." Who was she kidding now? She was so shocked and excited she could hardly stand up. Her blood didn't know which way to rush.

He brought her hand to his lips and bit down gently on the knuckle of her forefinger. The message in his eyes was explicit and unmistakable. He wasn't playing anymore. He wanted a woman and he meant to have one before he was through today. *He meant to have her.*

If she didn't stop him now, she would never summon the strength. He was too powerful, too physically overwhelming. But what disturbed her even more than the inevitability of his seduction was her own reaction. Some errant part of her *wanted* him to touch her again, to make her gasp.

She tried to deny the raw excitement that was coursing through her, but she couldn't close the floodgates. It was as though something wild and sweet inside her had been cut loose from its bonds, a trapped energy set free. She seemed to crave the dizzying, shocking feelings he evoked, as rough as he was, as primitive as he was. She didn't understand what was happening to her, unless it was the result of being emotionally immobilized for so many years. She was being catapulted back into life, into feeling things again.

He relaxed his fist and let her hair fall free, his fingers warm on her neck. "Have you ever made love on a kitchen countertop?"

"No," she said quickly, shaking his hand away.

"That's a serious gap in your education, Lace."

Before she could think of an argument, he'd picked her up by the waist and set her on the countertop. The chill from the tile penetrated the fabric of her slacks, and she reacted as though it were some kind of warning. She locked her legs together, shielding her breasts with her crossed arms.

"I've always thought the kitchen was the sexiest room in the house," he said, ignoring her defensive posture. "There's something basic and earthy about all the food, the stove, the sink . . . the *water*."

He reached around her and turned on the faucet, letting warm water bubble, trickle and run in a slow stream. Bev felt her stomach turning to liquid as she listened to it. Did he know she couldn't resist running water? She closed her eyes, trying to ward off the answering warmth that was stirring inside her. "You're not playing fair," she complained faintly.

"I'm not playing."

He ran his thumb nail slowly down the outside seam of her slacks. Bev felt her skin heat and blood race to the surface. A thrill of anticipation shot through her.

"Open your legs for me, babe," he said softly. "I want to get close."

Even the thought of opening her legs touched off an aching tightness in Bev's thighs. She could hardly move for the sudden, debilitating effect it had on her muscles. It was crazy what he did to her. He put her in a trancelike state every time he got near her. Her mind went into neutral and her body went into fifth gear. She was all raw nerves and stripped-down senses, vibrantly tuned in to her surroundings on some primal level. She could feel his hand resting near her knee, she could smell the crisp tang of lemon and hear the warm tap water running slowly, whirlpooling in the sink before it gushed down the drain.

He covered her knee with a hand large enough to completely engulf it. "What's it going to be, Lace? Are you going to unlock these beautiful legs anytime soon? Or are you waiting for me to do it?"

"*No*," she said, forcing herself to meet his eyes and push his hand away. "Nobody's unlocking these legs." The effort it took to resist him drained every last bit of strength right out of her. His features were so mesmerizingly dark, so demonically handsome, she couldn't have rallied the energy to hold him off again if she'd wanted to. She half expected him to pry her legs open himself and have his way with her right there in her kitchen. And maybe she half wanted him to! She didn't know what she wanted anymore, or even what she should want. Her thoughts were scattered and confused and she was shaking with excitement. All the fight had gone out of her. Surely he could see what he was doing to her?

Whether he could see it or not, Sam didn't act on it.

He shifted back, his hands still on her knees, and stared at her with powder-blue eyes that said he didn't know what the hell to make of women in general, this one in particular.

"You want it too, don't you?" His voice was as rough as sandpaper, the same whiskey rasp she remembered from their first meeting in the bar.

"I don't know," she said, completely sincere. She lifted a trembling hand to her throat. "Look at me, I'm shaking, I can hardly breathe. Maybe you should take *me* to a hospital."

"There are places I'd like to take you, babe, but a hospital's not one of them. Come here," he said, reaching for her.

Bev's arms shot up to stop him, but the rest of her body betrayed her. Her legs went tingly and weak as he hooked her by the back of the knees and brought her forward. She watched helplessly, knowing what was about to happen. A soft moan caught in her throat as he pressed into the V of her thighs and her legs opened automatically to accommodate him.

Cool air burned her warm, damp skin, and the sudden intimacy of the situation sent a shock of desire through her. She wanted desperately to slow him down, to regain some semblance of control, but she was dazed by the stormy excitement of it. The feelings intensified with every brush and jolt of his body against hers. And then, as his hips forced her legs to open even wider, the sensations became so sharp and exquisite, all she could do was gasp.

"God . . . you *are* sweet." He cradled her face in one of his huge hands, his fingers combing her hair as he bent to kiss her. Bev closed her eyes and felt his lips meld with hers in a throb of contact that deepened quickly into something heavier, hungrier. In the heat of the kiss he cupped her hips with his hands and scooped her forward. A low growl of pleasure came out of him as he brought her close, nestling her softness against his own burgeoning hardness.

Bev felt a shock wave roll over her. It flared up from that tender place where he was rocking against her, and then it ricocheted along her spine like the tremors of an earthquake. The sensation was fierce and dazzling, unlike anything she'd ever experienced before. It was pure, raw, physical sensation, and she lost touch with everything else but the staggering pleasure. She hadn't known that a physical sensation could seize hold of a woman so completely. No one had ever told her that the touch of a man's clothed body could sap a woman of willpower and drug her with the need for more.

"Dance with me, babe," he said softly, rocking against her. "Be my private dancer."

He slid his hands up her thighs, and the stimulation was so intense that Bev nearly fainted. She felt herself swaying backward, heard her own throaty laughter as he caught her by the arms and jerked her forward. Her head fell back, exposing her throat, and she knew instinctively that it was a sign of surrender.

"Dance with you?" she whispered, crazy for the sting of his lips on her throat. A strange urgency gripped her as she felt the pressure of his hips against her legs, felt the sweet, hot ache of her own thighs. Each thrust of his hardened body promised a deeper, more vital connection. She yearned for that connection; she burned for it.

Bev understood what was happening to her now. Finally she understood it completely. The sheer intensity of her responses to him had swept away any confusion. Trapped in an unresponsive body, her physical needs had broken free. They'd taken control of her senses, demanding nothing less than total abandon. She was making up for lost time, for years of denial and deprivation.

"Yes, dance with me," she breathed. "Now, here, wherever you want." She wanted him to tear off her clothes and make urgent, violent love to her, on the countertop, on the table, the floor. . . .

"Easy," he said, gripping her arms and holding her back. "One thing at a time, Lace."

Bev stared at him, confused. Her thoughts were spinning out of control. Had she been talking aloud? Had she actually said any of the things that were stampeding through her brain?

"The floor looks a little uncomfortable, but if you insist . . ."

His voice was stripped raw with desire, and his eyes seemed like black pools rimmed with silver. Taken altogether, he was the sexiest thing that Bev had ever seen. She felt a clutch of fearful excitement in her stomach, and she might easily have spun out of control again if it hadn't been for the faint smile pulling at his lips. Did he think this whole thing was funny? Was he laughing at her?

"I didn't actually mean the floor," she said, averting her eyes. "One tends to use figures of speech when one gets . . . carried away."

He brought her chin up, forcing her to look at him. "I like it when you get carried away."

The smile was gone, and his mouth was very near hers. For one fleeting second Bev wanted that fine, sensuous mouth on hers again—She tore her eyes away before the thought could take hold. *On the floor?* She'd begged a near stranger to have sex with her on the kitchen floor? Two naked people, writhing on her newly waxed linoleum? That wasn't possible.

The absolute certainty she'd felt in the throes of wanting him were drummed into submission by the guilty jolts of her heart. The urgent heat of her passion was cooling rapidly, leaving her shaken at what she'd done, and increasingly bewildered by why she'd done it. She stared into his turbulent blue eyes and felt as though she were sinking in a quagmire of confusion again. She barely knew who he was. She barely knew who *she* was.

"What are we doing?" she said breathlessly. "I met you only yesterday."

"Damn, I knew this was going to happen." The smile tugged at his lips again, and his voice went husky. "Lace, baby . . . don't go decent on me now."

"But I *am* decent."

"Yeah, but not too decent. You've got a wild streak in you, and I love it."

His fingers hardened on her face, refusing to let her turn away as he bent and brushed his lips over hers. "You wanted it, Lace," he whispered against her mouth. "You wanted it wild. And you wanted it from me."

Muscles pulled tight in the deepest reaches of Bev's body. It was true, everything he said was true. Dear God in heaven, she could hardly believe she'd let things get so far out of control. She'd barely lifted a finger to stop him. He probably thought she was leading him on.

That was then, she told herself. *This is now.* She'd lost control in the heat of the moment. It could happen to anyone—and probably did, all the time. But it had never happened to her before. Bev Brewster didn't beg men to make love to her on the floor. She didn't even date!

"I'd like you to move," she said abruptly.

"Why?"

So she could close her legs! He was still lodged between her thighs and she couldn't bear the way it made her feel. "This position. It's a little awkward for talking."

"Who wants to talk?" He touched her face, trying to seduce her again, with his ex-smoker's voice and his baby-blue eyes, but she wasn't having any of it.

"I do!" She caught him off guard with a mighty shove to his midsection, and as he stumbled backward, she slid off the countertop and made a dash for it.

"Now, just get that private dancer stuff out of your mind," she said, darting to the opposite side of the kitchen table from him. "Because you've got the wrong idea about me."

"I don't think so." He approached the table, blue eyes

flashing. The prospect of a game of kitchen-table tag obviously appealed to him.

"Stop right there, Sam!" She had to find a way to deter him. "This isn't right. It's . . . wrong."

"You're going to have to do better than that."

"All right, then, it . . . it's unethical."

"Unethical?"

"Yes," she said, realizing she'd hit on something. "Yes! It's unethical! You represent Mrs. Greenaway and I represent her husband. They hired us to investigate their spouses, and now here we are, kissing and stuff. That's a conflict of interest, don't you see. It's like . . . consorting with the enemy!"

He looked skeptical.

"I'm serious, Sam. Think about it. If either one of them found out, they could report us, pull our licenses."

He folded his arms, staring at her from under lowered brows. "Wasn't it you who said the Greenaways didn't need detectives?"

"Yes, but it isn't official yet. We haven't spoken to our clients, so we're still representing them." She pulled a deep breath, stood taller, and generously shouldered the blame. "I should never have brought you here, Sam. It was a serious error in judgment, and I'm going to have to ask you to leave now. Immediately."

He shook his head, an I've-heard-everything-now expression on his handsome face. "You've made your point," he conceded. "In fact, you've driven it through my heart like a stake, but don't kid yourself that this has anything to do with ethics. Even if you're right about the Greenaways, that isn't why you want me out of here."

Bev stared at him for a long time, her heart pounding. "I'll call you a cab," she said finally.

"Don't bother. I'll thumb."

She quickly darted past him, not allowing herself to glance back as she walked to the front door and opened it. A moment later she waved him through the door, immensely relieved as he left without further struggle.

"I don't think there's any need for us to see each other again," she said, shutting the screen behind him. "Our business is finished."

He swung around and grinned at her, a tornado of sexy virility. "I have a need, babe." His pale blue eyes held an even more explicit message. They told her that as soon as he had his client squared away, he was coming back for more.

A geyser of bubbles erupted in Harve's water glass as he tried to smother a chuckle and drink through the straw at the same time. He set the glass down, his wiry eyebrows bristling. "So this guy you clobbered yesterday? He turned out to be a private eye?"

Bev nodded, relaxing a little in the molded plastic chair. She was relieved Harve was taking the mixup in the Greenaway case so well. She'd kept the details to a bare minimum, leaving out the part about what had happened at her house afterward.

"Was he local?" Harve asked. "I may be laid up, but I still know everybody in the business. What was his name?"

Bev was eager to put the matter behind her. She had a meeting with one of the agency's most important clients the next morning, and she wanted to get some background information from Harve. Still, she knew he wasn't going to be content until he'd hashed over the Greenaway case to his satisfaction.

"He carried about twenty different IDs, but he called himself Sam Nichols."

Harve sat forward, his eyes lighting up. "*Sam?* Sam 'The Wild Man' Nichols? Hellfire! You're kidding me, aren't you, B.J.? I haven't seen that son of a gun in five years!"

"You know him?" Bev asked cautiously.

"Know him? He was my contact on the L.A.P.D. Hell of a good cop." Sam heaved a sigh and settled back on his pillow. "Shame he got shot up so bad. He left the force about six months after they released him from the hospital, just walked out one day and never came back. I heard the brass tried to clip his wings, make him a desk jockey. They never did like Sam's style."

He drifted off for a moment, smiling, obviously dwelling on better days. "Who's Sam working for?" he asked finally, leveling a glance at Bev. "Did he say?"

Bev shook her head. She couldn't imagine Sam Nichols working for anyone. "What did you mean when you said he got shot, Dad?"

"Cut down by machine-gun fire trying to stop a bank robbery. Now that I think about it, if it weren't for me, that boy wouldn't be alive today."

Bev sat forward, unable to quell her interest. The jagged scar on his jaw came back to her vividly. "You saved his life?"

Harve shrugged as though to say it was nothing. "Applied a couple of tourniquets to keep him from bleeding to death until the ambulance got there. I even visited him in the hospital, but do you think he ever thanked me? Hell, no. He didn't even bother to tell me he was quitting the force."

For all Harve's bluster, Bev could tell he was truly hurt by Sam's actions. The men must have had a strong bond at one time. "Maybe something was troubling him," she suggested.

"There was plenty troubling him," Harve agreed. "It wasn't a good time for Sam Nichols. He almost got himself killed, his wife walked out on him when he needed her most, and then there was that awful mess with his job—"

"Harve, let's talk about the Covington case," Bev cut in quickly. She had a hunch she was going to end up feeling sorry for Sam Nichols if she listened to any more, and she most emphatically did not want that.

Harve switched gears without protest, much to Bev's relief.

"Lydia Covington's got enough money to buy the U.S. Mint," he explained. "But she's a space case, ripe pickings for con men. She married some middle-aged Romeo a few months ago, and now he's skipped out with a chunk of her dough. She wants our agency to find him." He harrumphed disgustedly. "If she'd used our services before she married the hustler, we could have saved her the time and trouble."

Bev had been pondering the situation even as Harve talked. With him laid up and their two senior investigators gone, there was no one with enough experience to handle a complicated "locates" case. There would undoubtedly be travel involved—

"You're going to have to take this one, B.J."

Bev's head snapped up. He was going to trust her with something this important? "You think I can handle it? *Alone?*"

He stroked an eyebrow, deep in thought. "I think maybe Sam Nichols showed up at exactly the right time."

"What do you mean?" Bev rose from the chair, her heart beginning to pound. "Dad?"

"We need a senior investigator, don't we? Let's hire him."

"*No!*"

Harve squinted at her, surprised. "What's the problem?"

Bev began to pace. How could she get out of this? She doubted Sam Nichols would accept the offer even if she made it, which she had no intention of doing. But how to convince Harve that it was a disastrous choice?

"He's impossible, Harve," she said, talking as she walked. "He'd never fit in at Brewster's. He's arrogant and aggressive and competitive. He's not a team player, Dad." *And that's not all,* she thought. *He's a sex maniac.*

Harve chuckled. "Good ol' Sam. I'm glad to hear he hasn't changed. Oh, you'll get used to all that macho stuff, B.J. It's Sam's way. He was raised on the streets, and he's got some rough edges, but he's a damn fine detective. Trust me on this one, daughter, he's the best."

Bev stopped short, threw her hands up in the air, and groaned aloud. "Dad, read my lips," she said, turning to him. "I said it won't work. It's not me I'm worried about, it's the agency. He'd be a disruptive force. He'd have us all at each other's throats. So, forget it, okay? I can handle the Covington case on my own!"

Harve shrugged. "Cool your jets, girl. It was just a suggestion. We'll figure something out."

Bev was so busy fuming, she didn't hear her father's concession. Nor did she notice the glint of interest in his eye as he observed her flushed agitation. A thoughtful smile furrowed Harve Brewster's face, but Bev didn't see that either. If she had, she would have known she was in deep, deep trouble.

Five

Bev sat in her office listening to Lydia Covington's muffled sobs. Her client, a lovely, soft-spoken woman in her mid-forties, had just described how her husband of six months had bilked her out of half a million dollars in an investment scam, and yet now she was weeping openly because he was such a wonderful man. Bev didn't understand.

"But Mrs. Covington," she said gently, "he ran off with your money, a great deal of your money."

"Yes, I know," Lydia whispered brokenly. "I know what Arthur's done, but if you knew him, you'd understand." A shudder moved through her delicate shoulders. "My husband was a saint, Ms. Brewster, I swear it. Sweet-natured and sensitive, not an unkind bone in his body. And so good with the dogs. They loved him, my golden retrievers did."

She looked up, damp-eyed and forlorn. "Animals are a better judge of character than humans, don't you think? I keep wondering if there's been some mistake. Maybe Arthur's been taken hostage?"

Bev sighed. Lydia Covington wasn't being dramatic. She really loved Arthur Blankenship, the chiseler. What was worse, Bev had already done some checking, and it looked as though Lydia's husband was a bonafide con man. She couldn't tell her client that, however. Mrs. Covington was too fragile. She would fall apart.

Bev walked to Lydia's chair and knelt beside her. "I'll find him for you," she promised, taking her client's hand.

Lydia summoned what was left of her dignity. "Thank you," she said as the buzzer on Bev's telephone gave off several quick bursts.

Bev rose and pushed the intercom button. "What is it, Cory?" she asked the agency's young male receptionist. Cory was actually a student intern who was paying his dues at the front desk, the way all Brewster's investigators started.

"There's a man here to see you, B.J. His name is Sam Nichols, and he says it's urgent."

Bev glanced heavenward, summoning strength. "Tell him I'm busy, Cory." She smiled at Mrs. Covington over the receiver.

"He says you've got his sunglasses."

"I do *not*."

"He says you took them after you knocked him out yesterday. He wants them back."

Bev's heart sank. She'd set his glasses on an end table for safekeeping. Just her luck that she'd forgotten to give them back. She smiled at Mrs. Covington. "Take down his address, Cory. I'll have them sent back to him."

"Hey, what did you hit this guy with, B.J.? A sledgehammer? He's growing an eggplant on his head."

"His address, Cory." Bev replaced the receiver and turned to Mrs. Covington. "I've already done some preliminary work on your case," she said, stalling for time. She wanted to make sure Sam Nichols was gone before she walked her client out. "You met your husband on a Mediterranean cruise, didn't you?"

Mrs. Covington smiled wistfully. "Yes, Arthur swept me off my feet on that cruise. I'll never forget it."

"Well, I think I can assure you that Arthur hasn't been kidnapped. I ran a credit card check and it looks as though he's booked passage on another cruise in the Caribbean. My plan is to find him and then lure him back to the States. Once I've got him here, you can take whatever action you choose."

"I just want him to explain why he did it," she said softly, tears welling. She fished a hanky from her purse and blotted her eyes.

Bev felt a wrench at her heart. How could anyone have taken advantage of such a gentle soul? Suddenly Bev wanted to find Arthur Blankenship badly. Find him and make him pay. "You have every right to press charges, you know."

"Oh, no, please! I don't want the police involved. Not until I've heard Arthur's side of the story. I'm sure there's some explanation."

Like greed, Bev thought, watching the stricken woman tuck her hanky back into her purse. She could feel the bitterness rising in her throat. It was an emotion she'd never fully given vent to after Paul had left her. He hadn't stolen her money, but he *had* robbed her of self-esteem, and he'd nearly devastated her sense of herself as a woman.

Men, she thought, crunching down on the word. Her jaw was tight, her smile grim as she met her client's watery gaze. "You've got the right woman for the job, Mrs. Covington."

Bev returned to her office full of purpose after escorting her client out. The cruise ship left Fort Lauderdale the following evening and Bev planned to be on it. She didn't have a current photo of Arthur Blankenship. Understandably, he'd avoided having snapshots taken, but Lydia had given her an excellent description. Bev had also checked out the man's investigative file through her law enforcement contacts. He'd never been convicted of a crime, but complaints had been filed by other heartbroken women whose money he'd invested in questionable deals. Like Lydia, they'd refused to prosecute.

She was sitting at her desk, jotting some last-minute

notes, when she heard a rustling sound. As she looked up, the pencil she was using slipped through her fingers, rolled across the desk, and dropped to the floor. *"How did you get in here?"*

Sam Nichols was lounging on the couch where Lydia had been weeping only moments before, his booted foot propped on one knee, a toothpick dangling from his lips. "We're working together on this one," he said, the words little more than a husky whisper. "You've got a partner on the Covington case."

Bev shot out of the chair. *"What?"*

"If you're going to yell," he said calmly, "yell at Harve. This was your dad's idea. He saved my butt once. Now he wants me to return the favor"—he worked the toothpick expertly and flashed her a cheeky grin—"and save yours."

The urge to stomp, yell, and throw things nearly overwhelmed Bev. Normally she was even-tempered, but this man made her wild. He knew where her buttons were, and he couldn't keep his damn fingers off them!

"Harve shouldn't have done that," she said tightly. "I'm running the agency now. And your services are not needed."

He dropped his foot to the floor and leaned forward, propping his elbows on his knees. "It won't work, B.J. I owe your dad and I'm on the case whether you need my services or not. So let's talk about Blankenship. The sooner we find him, the sooner you'll be rid of me."

Bev sent her chair spinning backward with a bump of her hip, turned, and walked to the window. Apparently her father had already filled him in on the details of the case. Blast Harve anyway! Blast both of them. She wasn't obligated to work with Nichols if she didn't want to, no matter what Harve had cooked up, but the question was how to get rid of him. She was trying to think that through when his voice interrupted her train of thought.

"Harve's worried about you, B.J. He asked me to keep you out of 'harm's way'—his own words. He doesn't want you off globetrotting on your own, hunting down con men—"

Bev swung around. "So he's sending *you* along to protect me? The man who tried to ravish me in my own kitchen? Does he know about that?"

Sam looked her over, sitting back and taking his time, as though he were replaying the kitchen scene in his mind in great and graphic detail. His eyes brushed over her like a warm, steamy caress, and then he drew the toothpick from his mouth and snapped it between his thumb and forefinger.

"You won't have a problem with me, Lace," he said. "Not unless you want one. I'm doing this because an old friend's in trouble, not because I want to get into your undies."

She wasn't going to dignify his last remark with a comment, but her skepticism couldn't be contained. "Even Ripley wouldn't believe that one. You're saying you don't want to—" There didn't seem to be any safe way to finish the sentence.

"I'm saying my preference in women runs more to low-cut dresses than beige polyester slacks."

Bev's cheeks went hot. Apparently he was just making do yesterday. Killing time until a low-cut dress came along. She wanted to challenge him, but she refused to be put in the position of defending her own sex appeal. Ironically, he was the first man in years who'd made her feel as though she had any, which was probably why she'd been so susceptible to him.

"About the Covington case," she said, determined to get the matter settled.

"Here's the plan." He stretched his arms out in front of him and rose, much like a big cat awakening from a nap. "According to his M.O., Blankenship operates on cruise ships. We'll start with a credit card check, and then if necessary we'll check out passenger bookings on the luxury lines. Once he turns up, we've got him. You'll be the bait—a wealthy divorcee, a widow, heiress, whatever blows your skirt up."

"Bait?" Bev checked the zinger of a retort that came to mind. She stared at Sam, her disbelief fading as an idea glimmered and took hold. That was the oldest trick in the world, wasn't it? A woman as bait? The perennial mantrap?

Would it work?

It took a monumental act of self-control, but Bev sat back in her chair and forced a calm smile to her lips. Whatever unladylike urges she might have had to take Sam Nichols to task—even her secret desire to leapfrog the desk and smack the cocky smile off his face—were subdued in favor of the plan that was forming in her mind.

How could she smack the man who'd just given her two brilliant ideas? How to catch Arthur Blankenship. And how to get rid of Sam Nichols! "I'll be the bait," she said softly, already planning her strategy.

"You like that idea?" He seemed surprised.

She pretended to be considering it as she herded her runaway chair back to her desk and sat down. "It has possibilities. And by the way, there's no need to run a credit card check. I've already done it. Arthur Blankenship has taken a suite on a Caribbean cruise that leaves tomorrow."

"Yeah? That's great. Give me the details." Sam scooped her pencil off the floor and handed it to her, waiting as she jotted down the cruise line and departure information.

"Good work, boss," he said, his eyes sparkling as she handed him the note paper. "Pack your low-cut dresses."

"Oh, I will." Bev couldn't suppress a smile. It seemed a fair exchange, she decided, tapping the pencil against her desktop. He'd given her a wonderful idea. *And she'd given him the wrong cruise line.*

Bev didn't own any low-cut dresses. She'd picked up a backless Norma Kamali at Recycled Rags on her way home from the agency the previous day, and she'd borrowed several cocktail dresses and a bathing suit from her glamorous and very busty neighbor, Tina. Beyond that she would have to fake it.

Now, completely packed and waiting for the airport shuttle to pick her up, she hovered in her living room, fixated on the two small and rather silly material things she treasured most in the world: the "Bless This Mess" corkboard hanging above the wall phone that her mother had given her before she died, and the heart-shaped goldfish bowl where her only house pet swam contentedly, unaware that he was about to be abandoned.

"You're going on a Caribbean cruise, Bev," she whispered aloud. "Stop shaking."

Bev's devils of self-doubt had gone on a rampage the previous night, waking her up in the small hours of the morning and taking her prisoner until dawn. Like gremlins, they hid in the dark corners of her mind and sprang out at her when she was most vulnerable, keeping her awake all night, tormenting her with her own childhood fears of the unknown. Since her divorce they'd visited her often, reminding her of her failure, plaguing her with a newer, deeper sense of inadequacy.

For five years she and Paul had tried to conceive a child to no avail. They experimented with everything—charting her cycle, using herbs, vitamins, even fertility drugs. Tests showed there were no physical problems with either of them, but nothing ever happened.

Though Paul had never accused her directly, she knew he blamed her for their childlessness. It hurt, but she forgave him, knowing his frustration was as great as hers. Eventually she began to believe him and shouldered the blame entirely. That was when the feelings of inadequacy began. The day he left her, her world had collapsed around her, and she had retreated into a protective shell.

And now, this morning the sight of her own packed bags filled her with dread. Except to go to her dad's place and the detective agency, she hadn't been outside a sixty-mile radius of her own home in over two years. Until a month ago, she rarely left the house at all unless it was for necessities. Harve was right about the state of her isolation, she realized. She really had become a recluse since her divorce. And yet here she was, heading for the Caribbean to catch a con man. How had she gotten herself into this situation?

Perhaps Harve's resistance to her joining Brewster's had made her think of detective work as glamorous and exciting, filled with the allure of forbidden fruit. But that fascination couldn't explain her current predicament. She'd never acted on her impulses before. She'd never been that impetuous. Staring down at her locked hands, she thought about the nerve-racking excitement of the past few days, and the memories drove a painful shudder up her spine.

It was him, of course. Sam Nichols was the catalyst for her strange behavior. He'd triggered something dormant in her, a flame she'd thought long dead. He'd struck sparks. He'd caught her kindling pride on fire. And she'd fought back, rising to his challenges. She'd even won the last match.

Only now her nemesis was gone . . . and the flame had been extinguished by fear. They were all gone, she realized, in one way or another. Her husband, her father, Sam Nichols. She was truly on her own.

Warding off the icy stirrings of panic, Bev walked to the heart-shaped bowl that sat on her bookshelf. "Take it easy, Moby Dick," she said, tapping the glass. Her goldfish rushed to the source of the noise as though he expected to be fed. Bev sprinkled some extra flakes in the bowl, and as he darted to the surface, she dipped her hand into the water. "I hope Tina remembers to feed you."

He swirled around her finger, a streak of neon orange, and Bev felt her anxieties lessen. She'd bought Moby shortly after Paul left on the theory that a goldfish would be a safe companion for a woman in her state of mind. It had made an odd kind of logic then. She'd been afraid of what would happen with a cuddlier house pet, a snuggly kitten or a sad-eyed dog. She might have poured out all her pent-up love and longing. She might have become too attached. After years of wanting a child and having her husband leave her because she couldn't seem to get pregnant, Bev was afraid to get too attached to anything.

A horn sounded outside, and Bev knew it was the shuttle. It was ridiculous, but she didn't want to leave. She was afraid of what might happen to her so far away from home. She was afraid of what would happen to Moby if Tina forgot to feed him.

The horn blared again and she picked up her bags.

Sam Nichols drained the last beer in the six-pack, crushed the can in his hand, and tossed it onto the small mountain of aluminum collecting in the corner of his living room. "Garbage art," he said, pleased with himself as he considered the stack. "When it hits the ceiling, I'll hold a one-man show."

He crouched to stuff the rest of his gear into his duffel bag. It was the only luggage he planned to take, and he could already see Bev Brewster's disapproving glance when he showed up in chinos and a crewneck T-shirt. She probably expected him to wear flowered shirts, bermuda shorts, and put on one of those monkey suits for dinner.

"Why do women love it when a man's miserable?" he wondered aloud, easing the delicate surveillance equipment he'd just purchased into a separate zipper compartment. If a guy liked wearing jeans, they weren't happy until he was strangling to death in a starched collar and tie.

Sam had his own theories about men and women, including the deeply held belief that life had dealt women the ace hand where love and sex were concerned. A guy didn't have a chance in that high-stakes card game. Women made the rules, and they knew when to draw, when to stand pat, and when to bluff. A smart player wouldn't even sit down at the table. But hell, when were men ever smart when it came to sex? If a man wanted a woman bad enough, his glands took over. His muscles got hard, his brains got soft, and pretty soon he was playing her game—no-prisoners poker. Poor sucker knew he'd end up compromising his soul to have her. But he played anyway.

Sam gripped the duffel by its strap and heaved up, grimacing as he swung it over his shoulder. His right side was giving him grief today. Machine-gun fire did a heavy number on the human body, shattering bones, grinding muscles into hamburger meat. It had been five years, and he still didn't have the full use of his right shoulder and arm.

Luckily, his Mustang convertible was right where he'd left it the night before, parked across the street from the small El Monte apartment complex where he'd lived the past couple of years. The ragtop was a favorite among the neighborhood juvenile delinquents, who ripped it off regularly and went joyriding. Sam generally found the car a block or two away, wherever they dropped it off when the thrill was gone, but he'd never bothered to report the kids. He'd been raised on these graffiti-strewn streets. He knew the kind of families they came from, the chaos they lived in.

A hot wind whipped at Sam's dark hair and the neon-white spring sunshine nearly blinded him as he pulled onto the Long Beach Freeway, heading for L.A. International. His thoughts had returned to the female of the species several moments earlier, only he'd narrowed his focus down to one specific woman—Harve Brewster's daughter.

Life had dealt that one a wild card.

He smiled and hit the gas, dropping the car into third and pulling out from behind a meandering truck. Bev Brewster wasn't beautiful or sexy in any obvious way. At first glance it was hard to imagine a man losing his head over her, but she had a secret weapon guaranteed to twist a man's vitals into knots. Touch her and she went off like a bomb.

He laughed softly and switched on the radio, looking for a station that still worked. All that frightened, breathless passion was irresistible in a woman. She'd acted as though no man had ever set her on a counter-top before, as though no man had ever been between her legs.

He felt a sharp tug of pleasure in the pit of his stomach. He was going to have to watch his step with little Ms. Lace Collar. And not only because she was Harve Brewster's daughter. She was the type who sat down at the poker table and walked away with the whole pot. Beginner's luck.

The bon voyage party was still in full swing as Bev walked out onto the cruise ship's sun deck. She paused at the edge of the celebration and gave herself a quick once-over to make sure she wasn't exposing anything she shouldn't in Tina's strapless floral-print sarong. It was a Frederick's of Hollywood special with a built-in bra and push-up pads that made Bev feel as though she ought to be auditioning for a Las Vegas chorus line. She had never looked more voluptuous.

Slingbacks were mandatory for the "West Indies look," according to Tina. Bev was having trouble with her sea legs in the unaccustomed style, but she figured if she stuck by the rail and observed for a while, the odds of embarrassing herself with a fashion faux pas would be significantly lessened.

The party was a lively affair, with darting waiters dressed in lemon-yellow calypso shirts and a nine-piece steel-drum band playing in the shade of thatched um-brellas. The music's vibrant beat and shimmering me-tallic tones gave off waves of sensuality, inviting the laughing crowd to sway to its rhythms. Overhead, paper lanterns swung lazily in the trade winds like rainbow-colored necklaces.

Bev leaned against the railing, aware of the soft crash of waves behind her as the ship plowed through the water. The *Island Princess* had pulled out of Fort Lauderdale an hour ago, and now they were steaming toward the turquoise waters of St. Maarten. The cruise's itinerary featured ten islands, including some of the more remote and unspoiled Caribbean cays. If Bev hadn't been flirting with a panic attack, she might have been looking forward to it.

A waiter came by with a tray of frothy pink concoctions, and though Bev was sorely tempted, she refused. She'd paid a visit to the ship's doctor immediately after boarding and had a seasick patch applied as a precaution. She was already beginning to feel the side effects of the medicine—a touch of wooziness, a dry mouth—so she'd decided to avoid alcohol.

She began to circle the festivities slowly, staying at the periphery as she scanned the crowd for Arthur Blankenship. Lydia's description had made him sound rather average—medium height and build, brown eyes, prematurely silver hair—but Bev knew she was looking for a ladies' man.

The tables she passed were heaped with exotic hors d'oeuvres and platters of tropical fruit, but it was a punch bowl full to the brim with lemonade that caught Bev's eye. Curlicues of lime floated in the icy, pale yellow liquid.

She dipped herself a cupful. The drink was slightly tart and very refreshing. More like grapefruit juice than lemonade, she decided, but delicious. And she was absolutely parched. A moment later she'd drunk the first cup, poured herself a refill, and turned back to the crowd with a renewed sense of purpose. Even the knot of anxiety in her chest had unraveled a little. Now, where was Arthur Blankenship?

Bev found her quarry a short time later on the starboard side of the sun deck. The silver-haired, silver-tongued devil who had chiseled Lydia Covington out of *mucho dinero* was dancing with a redhead in a clingy denim bustier and miniskirt. So he'd traded Lydia for a high school dropout, Bev thought, loathing the con man on sight. The young woman was probably a temporary diversion. She didn't appear to have either the sophistication or the money that a pro like Arthur would automatically seek out.

Bev shook her head, letting her hair tumble around her face as she calculated her next move. She felt oddly warm and flushed, even a little giddy. Was it the seasick medicine making her feel so strange? she wondered, glancing at her nearly empty punch glass. The knot in her chest was coming undone like loose shoestrings. Under almost any other circumstances, she would have wilted at the prospect of a nubile younger rival, but some impulse was stirring inside her, urging her on.

She glanced at her saronged body and thanked the gods of lingerie for pushup pads. Her neighbor's fashion sense was to be applauded, she decided. Tina had promised the outfit would give her confidence. This must have been what she meant.

The steel-drum band launched into a faster number and Arthur and the redhead left the dance floor to stand by the railing. They were directly across the deck, and as they turned to gaze at the water, Bev decided to stroll their way.

She felt a flicker of vertigo as she set down her punch glass, and blamed it on her shoes. It wasn't until she was halfway across the dance floor that she realized something was truly out of kilter. Her hands fluttered in an odd dance as she hesitated, trying to correct the unsteadiness she felt. Reggae music blared in her ears and dancers swirled around her. And then the cruise ship itself seemed to roll beneath her feet.

She thrust out her arms to balance herself. "What's happening?" she said breathlessly. "Is this hurricane season?"

The dancers seemed totally oblivious to her plight. A

passing waiter ducked out of her way, leaving her to her own desperately dizzy devices. Another wave of vertigo caught her as the deck undulated beneath her feet. She started for a deck chair to anchor herself, but couldn't reach it.

"Help," she breathed, her arms flying out. Any movement on her part seemed to make it worse. She dipped and swayed like a belly dancer, her upper body going one way, her lower body the other. The other dancers still hadn't noticed her, but the spectators had. They were watching her as if *she* were the entertainment.

A heavyset man standing ringside flashed her a thumbs-up. "Show 'em how, lady," he called out.

Bev tried to shake her head, but it only made her dizzier. To her horror, the man began to dance toward her, shimmying his shoulders. "But I'm not dancing," she said as he dipped and bopped and boogied in her direction.

"Sure you are, gorgeous." He pulled her into his arms with a snap of his wrist. "With me."

Bev clung to him, terrified he was going to spin or dip or do something that would put them both in the hospital. "Over there?" She pointed toward Arthur and the redhead. "Could you dance me that way?"

Bev's heart sank as he locked his hips to hers and tossed his head like a bullfighter. Who did he think he was? Patrick Swayze in *Dirty Dancing*? She tried to push away from him, but he caught her by the hand and whipped her back into his arms as though it were part of their routine. And then he began to spin her toward the railing.

The crowd broke out in spontaneous applause, but Bev wasn't in any position to appreciate their enthusiasm. She felt like a whirligig in a high wind. She was twirling madly toward the railing when a man appeared out of nowhere, a phantom in a yellow shirt carrying a tray of drinks. As luck would have it, he was serving the redhead when Bev clipped him from behind.

"Look out!" someone cried as the waiter lurched

forward. The tray of drinks tipped, drowning the red-head in pastel bubbles.

Bev broke away from her partner and grasped the ship's railing, aghast as the tray and drinks sailed down the deck on a tidal wave of pink foam. Luckily the glasses were plastic. "I'm terribly sorry," she said. "The boat rolled or something. Did you feel it too?"

Bev turned to her partner, but he'd already spun off, probably in search of a better dancer. Clinging to the rail, she watched the redhead stalk off too, sputtering and crying, to change her clothes. And then, the next thing she knew, Arthur Blankenship himself was clasping her hand and asking if she was all right.

Bev knew she had to take advantage of the moment. "I'm fine," she said, smiling at him gratefully. In fact, she was dizzy as a top, her vision was oddly fuzzy, and she had a faintly metallic taste in her mouth. At least the ship seemed to have stopped rolling.

She clung to Arthur's hand for several moments, forcing herself to gather her wits as the dizziness finally began to subside. "Sorry about your friend," she said, glancing in the direction the redhead had gone. "Lovely girl. Your niece?"

Arthur flashed a quick, pained smile. "Just met her."

"Really? Very attractive," Bev murmured, releasing her death grip on his hand. "Very *young*."

"Jailbait," Arthur agreed absently, already caught up in the dazzling effect of Bev's strategically padded and underwired bodice. "Did you get wet?"

Bev summoned a provocative smile. "I'll never tell."

His eyes glinted hungrily, and Bev felt a moment of giddy triumph. He was lusting after her! And so quickly. That was pure, unadulterated male lechery in his eyes. She glanced down at her overflowing bustline and knew the reason why, but she hardly cared what his motives were at that moment. After years of feeling like a female eunuch, it seemed like the impossible dream. She'd actually had two men hot and bothered in less than a week's time!

Oh, this *is* fun, she thought. She'd been right about detective work. It could be glamorous and exciting. Not only that, the "bait" idea was working better than she'd dared to hope.

Arthur cupped Bev's elbow, spiriting her away from the scene of the crime as a crew of housekeepers appeared to mop up the spilled drinks. Bev glanced over her shoulder as they escaped, feeling a little guilty about the mess.

Once they'd found a quiet spot on the aft section of the deck, Arthur clasped her hand again. "My friends call me Tony," he said, playing with her fingers.

"Tony?" Bev didn't recall that alias from his police file, but then, con men changed names as often as their underwear. Probably more often in Arthur Blankenship's case. "My friends call me B.J.," she said, still a little breathless from their flight.

"I'll bet they call you other things too, B.J., like beautiful."

"The man's a poet." She laughed softly, the pleasure more real than feigned. Actually, Arthur Blankenship, the man of a thousand names, was much more attractive in a smarmy sort of way than Lydia Covington had given him credit for. Lydia hadn't mentioned how near black his brown eyes were or the way his teeth flashed when he smiled.

"Did you notice? It's a new moon tonight," he said.

They turned to look out at the water, and in the moments that followed, Bev lost count of the number of compliments Arthur lavished on her and simply allowed herself to laugh and enjoy them. She'd never been the type men went crazy over, and even though she knew it was all part of his come-on, it was still a heady experience.

"Something to drink, ma'am?"

A waiter paused beside Bev and she absently took a glass of champagne from his tray. "Thank you," she said, her eyes fixed on Arthur.

"Wrong guy." Bev felt a nudge from behind as someone whispered the words harshly in her ear. She nearly dropped her champagne. Who'd bumped her? The waiter?

He was gone by the time she got herself turned around. Puzzled, she searched the area and saw a man signaling to her through the crowd. Then she did drop her champagne. It was Sam Nichols in a yellow calypso shirt!

Bev gaped at Nichols's angry countenance as Arthur pulled her away from the spilled champagne.

"Are you all right?" Arthur asked. "You keep dumping drinks on the floor."

"I'm fine," Bev said haltingly. Her head was swimming with questions. Where had Nichols come from? How had he found her? "I'm sorry," she told the bewildered con man. "There's something I have to do. I'll be back as soon as I can."

Sam was moving among the guests with the drinks, but Bev could feel his eyes on her as she approached. There was no doubt that he was angry. The scar on his face was white, pulled tight by the tension in his jaw. Because of his size, he looked a little silly in pedal pushers and a calypso shirt, but any urge Bev might have had to laugh was smothered by caution. She didn't want to die.

"Thank you," she breathed, taking a drink off his tray as she reached him.

"Over there." He jerked his head toward a windscreen of fluttering palms near the stern of the ship, and then he left her, continuing to move through the crowd.

"What are you doing here?" she whispered a moment later as she joined him behind the potted palms.

His glare nearly melted the sarong off her body. "You're drunk as a skunk," he said incredulously. "And where the hell did you get that dress? Off a dead streetwalker?"

Bev bristled. This from the man who preferred low-cut dresses? "Well, thank you, Sam," she said tightly. "Arthur happens to think it's a lovely dress."

He jerked her around and pointed to the silver-haired man she'd been flirting with. "That's *not* Arthur, you little idiot."

"It is so!"

He turned her another forty-five degrees and pointed toward a small, bookish man with silver hair and wire-rim spectacles. He was standing alone, observing the crowd. "*That's* Arthur."

"It can't be—" Bev caught herself. She'd been about to say he didn't fit the description Lydia had given her. But, of course, a con man wouldn't. Arthur had obviously disguised himself with glasses and a more intellectual look.

"I think you'd better hightail it down to your cabin," Sam said, his hands tightening on her arms. "Before I lose my temper and do something that embarrasses both of us."

"What?"

His voice dropped to a harsh whisper. "Let's put it this way. I've never taken a woman over my knee in my life. I've never even thought about it . . . until tonight."

Six

Bev locked the door of her cabin and looked around in vain for a chair to prop up against it. Turn her over his knee? What rock had that man crawled out from under? Hadn't he heard of Gloria Steinem? Didn't he know that women were no longer bought and sold at slave auctions?

"Apparently not," she said, pacing the length of her tiny cabin. If he laid a hand on her, even one finger, she would—She folded her arms tightly and rocked forward, trying to think. Panic flashed through her anger, stopping her cold. What would she do? He was so damn big. He'd picked her up and set her down on her own kitchen countertop as though she were a bag of groceries.

She kicked off the slingbacks, her insteps aching. Life had become so complicated now that she had Sam Nichols to contend with again. He probably thought he was going to run the Covington case, but she had no intention of letting him push his weight around. As long as she was the bait, she would call the shots. If he wanted to take over, let him wear the falsies and lure Arthur Blankenship back to the United States.

She sank down heavily onto the bed, blotting the dampness from her neck as she considered her broom closet of a room. She'd booked so late she'd ended up with the last available cabin on the lowest deck. There were no windows, the air-conditioning didn't work, and it was so near the engine room, the constant drone made it difficult to think. And then there was the heat.

Perspiration was beading on her upper lip and in the cleft between her breasts. What she needed was a quick shower and some time to cool down before she had to face Mr. Tough Guy again. They'd established a pattern of catching each other off guard, so the next dance was hers.

She'd just about peeled herself out of Tina's sarong when she heard footsteps in the corridor outside her cabin. Someone twisted the doorknob, and she knew it was Sam. That man didn't have the manners God gave a donkey. Couldn't he knock?

"Just a minute," she said, thankful she'd remembered to lock the door. "I'm changing."

The doorknob jiggled again, a soft click sounded, and the door swung open. Bev grabbed a blanket off the bed to cover herself as the sarong slid to her ankles. Sam Nichols was leaning against her doorjamb, holding a toothpick between his thumb and forefinger. "These things come in so damn handy," he said quietly, his blue eyes flashing over her.

Bev wanted fervently to be angry with him, but he looked so outlandish in calypso gear, she couldn't get a good grip on her outrage. "I said I was changing."

"I didn't think you'd mind." He flicked the toothpick aside, seeming only mildly interested in the fact that she was wearing a blanket. "Especially since we're going to be sharing this cabin."

"I beg your pardon?"

For the first time that evening, Bev realized that his blousy shirt had no buttons. It tied at his waist and flowed open above to reveal swirls of panther-black chest hair, layered muscle, and . . . was that another scar?

"You've got yourself a bunkmate, Lace." The undersize

door frame forced him to duck as he entered the room and closed the door behind him.

Bev shook her head several seconds before the words made it out of her mouth. "I most certainly do not! Even if I were to entertain the possibility of such an arrangement—which I wouldn't—there is barely room in this cabin for me."

He leaned back against the door and folded his arms, the very portrait of an immovable object. "You're looking at a stowaway, babe. If you hadn't pulled that cute number with the cruise lines, I'd have my own cabin, and you'd have that bunk all to yourself." He nodded at the room's only bed. "I like the outside. How about you?"

"But there must be somewhere they can put you up? The crew's quarters?"

"Maybe you didn't hear me. I'm a stowaway." He raised his arm and tweaked the voluminous yellow sleeve. "I swiped this clown suit, and if they catch me impersonating one of their waiters, I walk the plank."

"What a delightful idea." She hitched the blanket up around her and stepped out of the sarong, bending to pick it up.

"Don't even think about blowing my cover," he said, letting his eyes coast over the most prominent point of her rather vulnerable position. "Or I may have to take that disciplinary action I mentioned."

Bev unbent immediately, glaring at him. "Don't be absurd! And don't you dare threaten me."

"Behave yourself, Lace, and I won't have to."

Their eyes locked. Bev felt her breath quicken as she held her ground. If this was another test of her mettle, Sam Nichols had better be prepared to back off. She would die where she stood before she'd let him do such an appalling thing.

"No man lays a hand on me and lives to talk about it," she said, breathing the words. "How could you be so base?"

"Me? Base? I wasn't the one drinking Caribbean

Kickers like they were water, dancing like Carmen Miranda, and knocking waiters on their butt."

"Caribbean Kickers?" Bev touched the patch behind her ear. "You mean the punch was—"

He nodded. "You were bombed, Lace. Admit it."

Bev sighed in exasperation. Did he have to be so blunt? At least now she understood why the boat had been rolling under her feet. And she also realized that Sam Nichols was doing it to her again. He was stirring up the banked coals, stoking the fire. She wasn't frightened anymore. She was angry, aflame. It felt good.

Sam saw the fire too. It was dancing in her gray eyes like quicksilver, molten flashes of mercury. It made her beautiful, and as hot as a Caribbean night. It drew him, that fire . . . but what drew him more was the earlier stirring of emotion he'd seen in her eyes. Fear, he thought, wondering if he was right. He rarely bothered looking below the surface. Most people weren't worth the effort, and he usually didn't like what he saw. But in this case he was fascinated by the deep whisperings of apprehension in her eyes. She was scared out of her mind about something. Was it him? Or just life in general?

"Just for the record," she said, her voice taut. "I don't care what you think of me or my tactics. I don't need your help, okay? I don't need anything from you. I may have messed up tonight, but I can handle this case—and I can do it alone."

Her show of bravado might have fooled someone else, but she had just confirmed Sam's suspicions. B. J. Brewster, only daughter of L.A.'s toughest private eye, was riddled with self-doubts. He was tempted to probe, but something told him her anxieties were rooted in concerns much more personal than detective work. On some level Sam could relate to her fears and the courage it took to face them. He'd done battle with his own demons for years—and the demons had won. She hadn't given up yet. She was still fighting.

As far as the work went, he could have reassured her

on that score. She was still wet behind the ears, but with a little more experience, she could handle anything she put her mind to. Her instincts were good, she just didn't know it yet.

He felt a softening toward her and abruptly forced it away. It was one thing to want her, but *liking* her, that was crazy. That was dangerous as hell. He had enough to deal with, keeping his physical drives under control.

"Whether or not you could handle the case on your own is beside the point," he said. "I'm here and I'm staying. That's the way your dad wants it."

Bev turned her back on him and threw open the lid of her suitcase. Arguing with a man without her clothes on put a woman at an unfair advantage, especially when that man was a practicing degenerate! Why did she have the feeling this was going to be just one of many times she would wish she'd hit him harder with her black-jack?

Under cover of the blanket, she slipped off her panty-hose and found a loose cotton sundress that would have to double as a nightgown if she couldn't come up with a way to get rid of him. When she turned back, he was pulling off his shirt. She was about to turn away again until she got a look at the scarring that had mutilated his upper torso. It looked as though someone had ripped at his flesh with a garden rake. The jagged marks rode a rough path from his right shoulder to his right hip. It was the closest thing Bev had ever seen to physical savagery, and her immediate impulse was to reach out to him, to comfort him.

She spoke softly, trying not to wince. "Is that pain-ful?"

He shook his head, but she could see the muscles working in his jaw as he forcibly wrenched himself out of the shirt. He didn't have full movement in his right arm.

"Was it the accident?" she asked.

His eyes flashed over her suspiciously. Bev sensed she was intruding, but somehow the sight of such devastation had made her forget their adversarial relationship. He was hurt and her heart went out to him just as it would have to anyone in his situation.

"My father said you'd been shot," she explained. "He didn't go into detail, just said that he was there, and that it was pretty bad. . . ." Bev let the words trail off, waiting for him to say something, to let her know that she was doing the right thing in pursuing it.

"Your father was there," was all he said. He glanced at his mangled shoulder and then at her for a long moment, as though he were trying to figure out her motives. Finally his hands dropped to his pants. He looked back up at her as he began to unbutton them. "I'm going to take a shower. You sure you want to watch this?"

Bev turned away. Apparently he couldn't handle sympathy. He seemed the sort of man who couldn't open himself up to any expression of emotion, and she thought that was a terrible waste. Something told her he might have been a different human being if not for the scars. But even as the words resonated in her mind, she realized she meant wounds that cut even deeper than the ones she'd seen.

She glanced around again as she heard his pants drop to the floor and saw him step into the shower. All she got was a glimpse of long, muscular legs swept with dark hair, but it was enough to confirm what she already knew. He was beautifully built. The machine-gun fire must have caught him from behind, she realized. The wounds she'd seen on his side and chest were caused by exit holes, by the brutal passage of too many bullets to count.

As she heard the shower come on, she forced her thoughts away from the damage to his body and began to think about rearranging the tiny cabin to accommodate two people. That she was capitulating so easily surprised her. She really was a patsy for a bird with a broken wing. Not that that description would ever fit Sam Nichols. He was more a battle-scarred panther, streamlined and treacherous, definitely not to be trusted as a house pet.

She was contemplating having him sleep standing up in the clothes closet when she heard an odd thumping noise.

"If I get stuck in this shower stall," Sam called out, "call the coast guard."

A panther with a sense of the ridiculous, she thought. Maybe there was hope. "Absolutely not. I'll let you turn into a six-foot-four prune."

"I'm only six three."

"You poor, puny thing, you." Smiling, she turned toward the stall and caught a glimpse of him moving inside the frosted plastic door. That she couldn't quite see any details made the sight so provocative. She couldn't pry her eyes away!

There was something beautiful about the deep flesh tones of his body against the smoky, soft-focus panel. It was like a dream image, a naked man moving through mists. Just when she thought she could see the line of his thigh, or the right angle of his hipbone, the image blurred and took new shape. Once she saw his shoulders flare out as he turned his back to her, and another time she saw the darkness between his legs.

Now, as she watched, the form moved fluidly in a kind of spiral as though he were turning in the spray. When he stopped, he was facing the door, facing her. He lifted one arm above his head, and Bev could see the inverted triangle of broad shoulders tapering to pelvis. A waterfall of dark hair streamed toward his groin, toward the wild black thatch and imposing male parts that drew the eye like a magnet.

Could he see her? Did he know she was watching him?

Her heart began to thud slowly—one hard, heavy beat at a time. Quite obviously, she was not immune to the physical charms of a naked man. And he was a whole lot of man, she admitted as she turned away.

The shower stopped, and she heard the door unlatch.

"Throw me a towel, would you?" he asked.

She had to walk past the shower stall to get him the towel, and it took a massive effort of will to keep her eyes from wandering to the open door. Now that she'd seen him in soft focus, now that her imagination had been cruelly stimulated, she wanted to see everything. All of him in graphic detail! She felt the same horrible fascination she had as a child when she heard frightening noises. She didn't want to look under the bed, but she couldn't help herself.

"Here," she said, thrusting the towel at him as his hand flashed out of the stall. "Did you bring any other clothes?" She wasn't sure she could deal with the calypso look much longer.

"There's a duffel bag in the closet behind you. I brought a wide assortment of jeans and T-shirts."

So he'd been in her room earlier, she realized, wresting the duffel bag out of the narrow closet. How could she have been naive enough to think she could escape him?

He emerged from the shower moments later, and Bev's first thought was that the towel knotted around his hips was several sizes too small for him. There were beads of water all over the parts of him that she could see, and she was immediately reminded of her problem . . . with wetness.

"Wouldn't you like to towel off and get some clothes on?" she suggested.

He shook his head as she pointed toward the duffel. "I think I'll drip-dry. It's hotter than hell in here."

"That it is," she agreed, wondering how she was going to get past him and over to the other side of the cabin. She didn't want to chance even the briefest contact with his dripping body.

He solved the problem by moving into the larger part of the room himself, the only area where there was enough space for two people to cohabit without touching. She followed him and sat on the farthest end of the bed.

Sam was well aware of the extremes she was going to to avoid him. "I suppose we ought to talk about this," he said.

"About the case?" Her smile was quizzical, as though she had no idea what he meant. "I'll make another run at Arthur tomorrow. I've got some ideas."

"About this." He indicated the cabin. "About us, in here."

"We'll make do. People have survived in worse circumstances."

Sam sighed. She was acting as though it was nothing, as though they were Andy Hardy and one of his girlfriends stranded on a raft. The way she was gazing up at him with her luminous gray eyes, he couldn't decide whether she was incredibly naive or exercising total denial.

She patted the bunk. "We can take turns if you want."

"Bev, Bev," he said, shaking his head wearily. "Time for a reality check."

"Reality check?" Bev didn't like the sound of that.

He reached her in one stride and Bev expected to be pulled off the bed to her feet. She scooted back as he knelt in front of her and rested his hand on her knee. If only he weren't such a large man, she thought, feeling a wave of helplessness as his hand dwarfed not only her knee but her leg. If only she were a bigger woman, a stronger woman, a *better* woman.

The memory of their steamy interlude in the kitchen began to screen through her mind, and she locked her legs together. She couldn't let that kind of wantonness wash over her again.

"Remember how this worked?" he said, drawing her toward him.

Bev felt her legs give way as he pressed between them, her dress sliding up. She knew instinctively she would be lost if he got that close to her again. She couldn't let him near her inner thighs. There was something about having him lodged between her legs, his hipbones pressed up against the exquisitely sensitive nerves and muscles, that shut down all her inhibitions.

"Only we never got to this part, did we?" he said, stroking her jawline with his fingers. He tilted her head up and brushed his lips across hers. "We never got to the kiss," he murmured as though the idea of a kiss with all its tender possibilities surprised him.

Bev was surprised too. In fact, the sheer lightness of his mouth as it moved over hers, the breathy, sexy warmth of him, was so unexpected that she relaxed her guard for a second. And with that tiny capitulation, her body went crazy. Her heart began to race, and she emitted a soft sound, not a sigh, more a surrendering of the breath stored in her lungs.

His hand tightened on her upper arm.

"Don't make noises like that, Lace," he said against her mouth, his voice raspy. "Not unless you want me to take your sweet body here and now." He urged her closer, lifting her up to him as he deepened the kiss. She could feel the wild sexual pull in him, the need to crush her in his arms, to drag up her skirt and drive himself deeply inside her.

She could feel the answering need in her own throbbing pulsebeat—the one in her throat, the one deep inside. What kind of strength did it take for a man to hold back when he sensed that a woman wanted him? When that same foolish woman melted under one tender kiss? When she throbbed every time he spread her legs?

"Come here, Lace." He caught her by the backside and dragged her up against the part of him that throbbed too. The sudden heat, the unyielding hardness, made her whimper.

"God, do I need to get close," he said harshly.

But, seconds later, when he had her firmly pressed against him and when he had her so aroused she couldn't say her own name, he drew back. His breath was ragged, his features hardened, ravaged by desire.

"See what I mean?" he said, touching her face. "See what I mean?"

He released her all at once and pushed back, taking a moment to catch his breath.

Bev was staggered by his ability to cut himself off. She was panting as if she'd run a mile uphill, her heart roaring in her ears, and worse, there was a deep, clutching ache in her nether regions that felt as though it would never let up. How had he done it? How had he stopped?

She felt a flash of anger, at him for having that kind of control, but more so at herself for being weak and ineffectual, a slave to her own raging hormones. She wanted to berate herself endlessly, but she couldn't stay focused. She was too fascinated by what was happening to his towel as he rose to his feet.

The knot that held it on his hips had loosened, and for one breathless second she thought the towel was coming undone. Her heart went wild at the prospect of seeing him that way. Her stomach lurched, and she felt a shuddering wave of disbelief at what was happening to her. She wanted to gawk at an aroused naked man. She must be going crazy!

"The towel!" she said, her voice a squeak.

He caught it before it came loose, and Bev hunched over on the bed—relieved, disappointed, horrified! She squeezed her eyes shut, jerked her dress down, and moaned. She wasn't going crazy, she was already there. She was a fruitcake!

The bed moved as he sat next to her, and she turned away from him, curling into herself. "Don't touch me."

"I was making a point, Lace," he said, his voice surprisingly gentle. "We're hot for each other. It isn't going to be easy, staying in a cracker box like this. We could be on each other constantly, going at it like rabbits. Is that what you want?"

Going at it like rabbits? Good grief, he was crude. "Why do you suddenly care what I want?" she asked, uncurling to look over her shoulder at him. "You didn't the other day in my kitchen."

He groaned softly. "Because you're someone's daughter now—Harve's daughter. And because I'm an idiot!"

She met his eyes and they held one powerful message. In spite of his promise to her father, Sam Nichols wanted to strip her naked and throw her back down on the bed. Well, maybe that would be the best thing, she thought, her heart pounding recklessly. Maybe they'd get it out of their systems. "I don't report to my father," she said, folding her arms. "Not about my personal life. I've been married, divorced. I do what I want."

His baby-blue eyes went dramatically dark, and his harsh breath brought her back to reality with a start. What was she trying to do? Talk him into attacking her? A quick perusal of the situation, of the tiny cabin and his still-aroused body, persuaded her to go cautiously. Another awareness drove that cautiousness home. She would be incredibly foolish to let herself get causally involved with Sam Nichols. She hadn't yet had time to analyze the reasons, but she knew that she could get very attached to a man like him. He had all the right stuff—dark good looks that made him physically irresistible, scars that tugged at her emotionally.

She took a deep, steadying breath. "All right," she said finally. "I guess we need some ground rules. First, clothes. I don't think we ought to be parading in front of each other half naked, do you?"

"Consider it done." He rose and crossed the room to his duffel bag, letting the towel fall as he pulled a pair of jeans out of the bag. Bev closed her eyes before she could get a good look at his muscular backside. She was learning.

Once he had the jeans on, he turned back to her and dug a silver dollar out of the front pocket. "Sleeping arrangements," he said, his eyes glinting mischievously. "Who gets the bunk? Want to toss for it?"

"Heads," Bev said instantly.

The coin went sailing up in the air, flashing as it

arced and dropped back to earth. Sam caught it and slapped it onto the back of his hand. "Tails."

Bev moved in for a closer look. It *was* tails, big as life. She glanced down at the woven carpet. "Well, I meant to say that," she said softly, looking up at him. "I meant to say tails."

"Too bad you didn't." Laughing, he pulled both pillows and the blanket off the bed and handed them to her. "Here, you can have these, babe. Don't say I never gave you anything."

Maybe he *was* resistible, she decided, giving him the full benefit of her contemptuous glare. Yes, he definitely was. He was rude and crude. And he still didn't have the manners God gave a donkey.

Bev would never have gotten an argument from Sam about the deplorable state of his manners, but she might have been surprised to know that his conscience was in fair working order. Fortunately, he'd always been able to ignore the small voice in his head when it stood in the way of getting something he wanted. But with her, he was having some trouble finding the off button. Must be because of Harve, he told himself.

He rolled to the side of the bunk and studied the figure curled up in the fetal position on the floor. Beverly Jean, he thought, contemplating her name, B.J., babe, Lace. She was the cuddly type, a woman who brought any number of pet names to mind. She was hot-blooded too, which never failed to surprise him. But her body heat wasn't what concerned him at the moment. It was the anguished little sighs she made as she tossed and turned.

He wasn't quite egotistical enough to think it was leftover passion. She was trying to get comfortable on the floor, and she was probably going to keep both of them up all night in the effort.

"Come on up here," he said. "There's room for both of us."

"Oh, sure," she bit back. "I'll bet you'll even let me choose whether I want to be on the top or the bottom, right?"

"Hey, who mentioned sex? I'm talking about getting some shut-eye, okay? Just sleep, nothing sweaty."

"No thanks," she said coolly, turning away from him. "I'm fine."

He exhaled heavily, swung off the bed, and bent to scoop her up. She stiffened like a board when he touched her, making his task that much more difficult.

"Don't you dare," she said as he worked his hands beneath her rigid body. Pain ripped through his side as he lifted her and rose to his feet, all in one gut-wrenching motion. It took a brutal determination not to drop her as frayed nerves and straining muscles screamed at him.

"Lighten up," he said, clenching his jaw. "I'm trying to do something nice. Don't make me regret it."

He deposited her on the bed and sank down beside her, his forehead filmed with perspiration. Something told him this wasn't going to be the last time she would bring him pain.

"Are you all right?"

"Yeah, I'm just great," he said, flinching as she touched his shoulder.

"I'm sorry. Is there anything I can do?"

The softness in her voice, the concern, seemed to make everything hurt more. "Lay down, dammit," he growled, not meaning to be so surly. "Go to sleep."

She moved away from him, pressing up against the wall. She was obviously apprehensive, but he didn't have the energy to reassure her, or the desire. Try to be a Boy Scout, and this is what you get for your trouble, he told himself. If she hadn't figured out yet that Sam Nichols was one nasty package, then maybe it was time she did. It was the way he'd grown up, the way he'd survived growing up. She'd get used to it, and if she didn't . . . well, that was her problem.

He stretched out on his back and stared at the ceiling,

wishing like hell he were in his rathole of an apartment with a six-pack of beer, drinking himself to sleep.

She lay down finally, on her side, staring at him. "Sam, I know you're hurting. I've got some aspirin in my bag." She touched his arm lightly, tentatively, a sweet promise of something more. "Would that help? Sam?"

He could hear the apprehension in her voice, the catch of emotion. She was frightened of letting herself get too close to him. She knew as well as he did what happened when they got close. They went crazy. They blew the fuses and shorted out the circuits. But there was something else happening between them too, a strange new urgency . . . a need to touch and discover, a need to make contact.

He could hear it in her voice. And he could feel it taking shape deep inside him, grabbing hold like a fist. He could feel it . . . and it scared the holy hell out of him.

Her fingers hovered on his arm. "Sam?"

"Get some sleep," he said abruptly. "You've got to bag a con man tomorrow."

Seven

Do they have chiropractors on cruise ships? It was the first question to filter through Bev's slumberous thought processes as she woke up the next morning. Her muscles were stiff and achy from the cramped position she'd slept in. Her spine felt as though it would never unkink. She moaned softly and rolled to her side, contemplating the wrinkled sheets where Sam Nichols had slept next to her the previous night.

It was another moment or two before it dawned on her that she was alone in the cabin, that Sam had already gone out. Did that mean he was a morning person? she wondered, gingerly stretching her arms and legs. Another bad sign. She was a night person. It was probably the only bohemian aspect of her entire personality, and she couldn't believe it was the one vice Sam didn't have. If he was the type that rose with the birds, they were truly incompatible.

She propped herself up on one elbow and considered the possibility of actually sitting up. She didn't want to rush her body into a vertical position, especially after the night she'd had. Sam's jeans were draped over the chair at the foot of the bed, which meant he must be wearing the calypso gear again.

By the time she was on her feet and mulling what she

was going to wear that day, she'd come to a couple of conclusions about Sam Nichols. His sexual prowess and his cynical sense of humor were obvious. He was also a profoundly private man. It was hard to imagine him as sensitive, or vulnerable in any way, but what else could account for the way he guarded his emotions and turned surly when someone got too close?

In his own way he'd been reaching out to her the night before, she realized. The offer to share the bed had been his way of extending himself. She could only guess at what it must have cost him to come out from behind his tough façade, even briefly. The roughneck with baby-blue eyes, she thought, smiling. Did he have a soft side? Was it his own tenderness he was protecting?

She felt a welling of sympathy. If she was right about him, he was sorely in need of someone to talk to, someone who cared enough to probe for the real Sam Nichols. But would he ever allow it?

She'd taken her shower, dressed, and was putting the finishing touches on her makeup before she realized she'd spent the entire morning thinking about her bunkmate. She would have to watch that kind of preoccupation. It could get dangerous, especially if she was wrong. What if the tender side of his nature was only wishful thinking on her part?

With one eye closed, she applied a liberally glued false eyelash, and a guilty smile appeared as she thought about Sam's reaction to her sarong the night before. He hadn't seemed too receptive to her sex-bomb look. In fact, he'd been downright insulting.

So let him stew, she told herself. The things Sam Nichols didn't know about her would fill a book. He had no idea how long it had been since a man had looked at her with anything but polite disinterest in his eyes. Or how badly she needed to be appreciated for her femininity. Perhaps she hadn't fully understood those things herself, until this trip.

She winked at herself in the mirror, testing the eyelash. "Lookin' good," she murmured. Moments later she whisked up her purse and left the cabin, a jaunty swing in her step. With her eyelashes attached and her pushup pads in place, she felt bold, a woman who knew her way around the promenade deck. If Sam Spade took exception, she would just have to remind him that the bait idea had been his.

Bev found the object of her search near the pool having brunch. Arthur Blankenship sat at a table by himself, absently buttering a croissant as he read silently and avidly from what appeared to be a popular novel. He was so engrossed he didn't notice her strolling by him, even when she paused and glanced over his shoulder to get a look at what he was reading.

Haunted Summer. Interesting choice, Bev thought. She hadn't read the book but she was familiar with it from college, where she'd briefly majored in English before dropping out to marry Paul. The story, as she recalled, was a rather erotic account of the weekend that Lord Byron, Percy Shelley and his wife, Mary Shelley, had spent one summer at Diodati, Byron's villa in Geneva, Switzerland.

Bev glanced around the deck to make sure she wasn't noticed, and then she casually bumped the back of Arthur's chair, hoping he wouldn't recognize her as the dancing dervish of the night before. He didn't even look up, so she nudged the chair again, harder.

Again, no response. Was he awake? Alive?

Perplexed, Bev stood back to rethink her strategy. The obvious solution was to tap him on the shoulder, and she was about to do that when he glanced up and saw her.

"Oh!" he gasped, lurching forward as he tried to stand up. The book caught the edge of his saucer and tipped over his coffee cup, which fortunately was nearly empty.

"I'm sorry," she said quickly. "I didn't mean to frighten you." Sweeping the napkin off his lap, she blotted the spilled coffee. She was making a career out of serendipitous accidents. "I hope your book didn't get wet."

"N-no, I don't th-think so."

Bev picked the book up. "*Haunted Summer*?" she exclaimed. "Where did you ever find a copy? I've heard it's marvelous."

Arthur jerked his head up almost painfully, as though he'd been caught at something. "I b-beg your pardon?"

"Isn't this the story about Shelley and Byron? I love Shelley's work, don't you? 'And we sail on, away, afar, Without a course, without a star.' That's from *Prometheus Unbound*. Lyrical, isn't it?"

"Why y-yes, it . . . is."

Bev hesitated, suddenly aware of her subject's discomfiture. Arthur Blankenship, the alleged lady-killer, was blushing furiously. He even had a slight nervous hesitation in his speech. She was almost sorry she'd disturbed him. Beyond that, she had the craziest impulse to pat his hand and tell him that everything would be all right.

"Oh, this *is* wonderful," she said, returning the book to him. "I know so few people who appreciate the romantic poets. I wonder if we might, well, I mean, if you'd ever like to discuss iambic pentameter or anything."

He nodded and indicated the chair next to his. Bev sank down, immensely relieved that he was following her lead. "I don't know if you'd consider loaning me the book when you're finished," she continued, aware of his brown eyes blinking behind the spectacles. They were enormous, and rather soulful. "I would guard it with my life."

"Please," he said, pushing the book toward her.

"Oh, thank you! Are you sure?" Bev had a tendency to talk when she was nervous, which she was at that moment. She launched into a monologue that quickly threatened to exhaust her modest knowledge of the romantic poets. Fortunately, Arthur made a gallant effort to save her as she began to run out of material. He was knowledgeable about both Shelley and Byron, their work and their legends, and the more he talked, the more he seemed to warm up to the subject. He actually smiled at her several times without blushing, and his speech was less halting.

"You know, you look a little like Mary Shelley," he said, contemplating Bev's features. "Of course, she didn't have your extr-extraordinary gray eyes."

"Why, thank you." Bev was truly flattered. Though she couldn't summon a mental image of Mary Shelley's looks, she knew the woman was considered beautiful in her time.

"Would you like some- something?" Arthur asked, waving for service. "Coffee? A croissant?"

"Oh, no—" But it was too late. A waiter was already on his way over to them. And this particular waiter happened to be wearing a yellow calypso shirt and a familiar glower.

"Please bring this inordinately lovely creature whatever she'd like," Arthur said without the slightest hesitation. He smiled up at Sam Nichols, seemingly undaunted by their waiter's looming presence.

Bev was not undaunted. Sam didn't look as though the night had improved his opinion of her tactics. His smoldering blue gaze moved over her, nearly setting fire to her eyelashes. She brought a hand to her breasts, covering herself protectively.

"What would the *inordinately* lovely creature like?" Sam asked, an eyebrow arching.

"Coffee," Bev said quickly.

"No Caribbean Kickers today?"

"Just coffee."

"Cream? Sugar?" Sam pretended to be jotting something on his tablet. "A bib for the lady's chest?"

Bev shot him a warning glance.

Arthur pursed his lips, apparently contemplating Sam's menu of questions. "I think we'd both like a bib, wouldn't we?" He smiled at Bev. "Are they cruise souvenirs or something?"

Sam's eyes narrowed. "If it's a souvenir you want—"

"Just coffee." Bev breathed an inner sigh of relief as Sam snapped his head in a military nod and left without any further discourse. However, it did strike her as odd that Arthur seemed to be so interested in Sam's departure.

"Is something wrong?" she asked.

"Strangely enough, he reminds me of someone too."

Bev felt a moment of alarm. A con man and an ex-cop? It wasn't impossible that he and Sam had crossed paths. "Really?" she said. "Who?"

Arthur pursed his lips contemplatively. "Byron, I think."

"Lord Byron?" Bev tapped the novel. "This Byron?"

"Umm . . . yes. Although the poet was much shorter, of course, and had a noticeable limp. But then, our friend has a limp too, doesn't he?"

Arthur nodded in Sam's direction, and Bev spun around to look. There was a slight catch in his stride, probably because of the shooting, Bev thought. Or maybe he really had hurt himself last night.

"Dark and melancholy, given to rages, Byron was," Arthur went on conversationally. "You know, he was supposed to have had an affair with Mary Shelley. It's all in the book."

Bev found herself tapping the novel again. "This book?" She was beginning to sound like a parrot.

Arthur was thoroughly enjoying himself by the time Sam returned with the coffee. Recounting the scandalous details of Byron's love life had brought color to his pale cheeks and a devilish twinkle to his brown eyes. "Women couldn't resist him, lucky dog," he said, leaning over to Bev conspiratorially. "They called him the demon lover."

"Demon lover?" Bev's voice was more animated than she'd intended. Apparently Arthur had infected her with his avid enthusiasm. "Really? He must have been—"

"Kinkier than a pretzel," Sam muttered, setting Bev's cup of coffee in front of her.

"Look who's talking." Bev breathed the words and laughed brightly as she reached over to touch Arthur's hand, hoping to distract him from their waiter's surliness.

Arthur's smile was pure bliss.

"Anything else?" Sam bit out.

"Some privacy?" Bev murmured.

Sam didn't budge. And finally Bev was forced to look up at him. "Cream," she said instantly, blanching under his dark scrutiny. "Could I have more cream?"

"By all means," Arthur chimed in. His expression was rapt and eager, as though no other woman on the deck existed but Bev. "More cream for the beautiful lady."

There was nearly an unfortunate accident when Sam returned with the cream. In fact, if Bev hadn't been on her toes, the cream pitcher would have landed in Arthur's lap. "Look out!" she cried, jumping up as Sam's tray tipped and the pitcher began to slide. She caught the edge of the tray and righted it, but not before some of the cream had slopped over.

"Look what you've done." She fired an accusing glance at Sam as Arthur fumbled with his napkin, trying to clean up the stains on his pants.

"The boat must have rolled," Sam said, borrowing Bev's excuse of the night before. "And by the way, *ma'am*, you have a phone call. Would you like to take it at the table? Or should I bring the phone to your *cabin* where you can talk *privately*?"

Bev spotted his ploy immediately. There was no phone call. He wanted to get her alone so he could read her the riot act. "I'll take it at the table," she said.

"No! No, my dear," Arthur insisted. "I have to go and change anyway. Please, take the call in your room." He nodded for her to go. "Perhaps we can meet for lunch? Or dinner?"

"How about lunch *and* dinner?" Bev barely got the words out before Sam had pulled back her chair. She rose abruptly, teetering as she made a grab for Arthur's novel. "The Promenade Deck?" she said, tossing Arthur a hurried smile as Sam led her away. "Half an hour?"

"What's this all about?" Bev said under her breath as Sam hustled her down the stairway to their cabin. She was trying her best to keep up with him, tuck the book into her tote bag, and avoid taking a header down the stairs, all at the same time.

"We need to talk about standard operating procedure."

"There's nothing wrong with my S.O.P."

Sam twisted the key, shouldered open the door to their cabin, pulled Bev inside, and shut the door behind them. "The first rule of detective work," he said, grinding out each word, "is don't *ever* let it get personal."

Bev tossed her bag on the bed. "What does that mean?"

"It means you're getting emotionally involved. You *like* that jerk. I can see it in your eyes. The way you smile at him, the way you laugh and . . . blush, or whatever flaky things women do. Hell, Bev, you're acting like a dizzy teenager on a first date. And so is he!"

"Well, isn't that the point? I'm supposed to lure him into a relationship and—"

Sam cut her off in exasperation. "Have you forgotten who Arthur Blankenship is? He's a rip-off artist, a swindler!" He raked a hand through his dark hair and glanced up at the ceiling as though looking for divine guidance. "I don't get it. What do you see in that dork anyway?"

"Wait a minute." Bev was beginning to get the picture. This wasn't about her S.O.P. She gaped at Sam for a moment, and then a smile broke. "Are you—oh, I don't believe this! Are you actually jealous of Arthur? Of that sweet little man?"

"*Sweet little man?* Listen to you. You're proving my point, babe. You're defending a con man." He hesitated, squinting at her suspiciously. "What do you mean . . . jealous?"

"Well, are you?"

"Hell, no! Get serious! That's about the dumbest thing I've ever heard." He turned away from her and slapped a hand against the wall above his head, as though he needed to support himself, the idea was so ridiculous. "Jealous of that Nerf ball? That'll be a wet day in the desert." He pushed away from the wall abruptly. "I've got to get back to work. I can't deal with this."

For several seconds after he'd left, Bev simply stood there, staring at the door, puzzled and secretly pleased. He *was* threatened by Arthur, even if he wouldn't admit it. But what did that mean? she wondered. Did it mean that he had feelings for her beyond the obvious sexual attraction? Or was it simply territorial instincts? Laughter bubbled so spontaneously, she couldn't control it. Sam Nichols was adorable when he was jealous.

The door swung open again, and Bev jumped backward.

Sam stood on the threshold, staring at her for several seconds. Without a word he stripped off the calypso shirt and strode across the room as though he was going to change his clothes. He yanked his duffel bag out of the closet and turned back to Bev, the confusion in his eyes completely sincere. "I don't get it, okay? I just don't get it. What is it about Arthur Blankenship that turns you on?"

A pulse ticked hotly in Bev's throat. "What makes you think he turns me on?"

"Does he?"

She gave herself a moment to think about it, and to recover her composure. "Well, yes, in a way," she admitted. "There is something sweet about him, and I think most women find that appealing in a man. He's not afraid to be vulnerable, to show his tender side. You'd probably call that wimpy, but I think it's brave." She gave Sam a meaningful look, and hoped he got the point.

He got it, all right, but he didn't seem to like it. "Correct me if I'm wrong," he said, sarcasm evident in his low tone, "but I thought women liked their men strong. I thought a woman liked it when a man knew what he wanted . . . especially if what he wanted was her."

There was such intensity in his voice that Bev's heart began to pound erratically. "Of course women want strong men," she agreed, "but it isn't an either/or situation. A man should be in touch with his strength *and* his vulnerability. I think a woman wants a man who can talk to her, a man who can—"

The closet door slammed shut, cutting her off. Sam released the latch slowly and turned to her. "A man who can do what?" he said, his voice dangerously low. "Make her *feel* like a woman?" He caught Bev's gaze and held it. "You're the expert on what women want. What about you? What do you want?"

He walked toward her, and Bev felt as though the room were closing in around her as he neared. The scar drew at his mouth, pulling sensually at his lower lip. His eyes had gone dark, and they were beautiful with their flashes of anger and desire. He was a thrilling man, a frighteningly powerful man. But there was another quality hidden in his features that pinned Bev like a butterfly to the mat. It was a shadow of something she might have read as hunger in a more accessible man. Did he have longings? Did he need something from her that went beyond sex?

His hand flashed up, reaching out for her. And then he checked himself. "What *do* you want from a man?"

His hesitation took Bev by storm. He'd obviously wanted to touch her, to pull her into his arms and kiss her, or ravish her, or something—but he hadn't. He'd held back, and the thought of him harnessing all that turbulent energy made her feel strange inside, breathless.

"I don't know," she said, suddenly remembering his question. She truly didn't know at that moment. Her head was spinning, her thoughts jumbled.

He unclenched his hand and reached for her again,

slowly. Bev closed her eyes, expecting force. Instead, he touched her eyebrow, just at the sensitive ridge where it arched and feathered out.

"Yes, you do, Lace." He explored her face with the pad of his thumb, following the crest of her brow, arcing over her cheekbone and into the hollow that curved toward her lips. "You know everything you need to know." It was the lightest, most arresting sensation Bev had ever felt. It tingled her skin and set her mind on fire. It made her anticipate the moment when the lightness would give way to something deep and raw and passionate.

What did she want from a man? She wanted safe passage from Sam Nichols at that moment. She didn't dare let herself think about anything else she might want from him, or they'd never get out of the cabin. "No . . . I don't," she insisted, turning away, pretending to straighten her dress. Her heart was beating so heavily, it hurt.

"Then maybe I can help you out."

Bev didn't want his help, and she certainly didn't want to hear what he had to say, but his pause forced her to wait, to listen.

"You like it when a man comes on strong," he said finally. "You like to be kissed until you're dizzy, Lace. You want a caveman . . . or at least you did yesterday."

She shook her head, warding him off. "That was yesterday. No!" she cried dazedly as his hand combed into her hair and brought her around to face him. "No, don't do that again."

"Don't do what?" Catching her under the arms, he picked her up and set her on the dresser top, gathering her close. His hipbones pressed into the side of her thigh and his hands were rough and thrilling. She could feel them burning through the cotton material of her sundress. "Don't do this?" he said, running his hands up her midriff to just below her breasts. "Don't touch you like this?"

There was raw passion in his voice, raw passion in

the way he curved his hand to her jaw and brought her face up to his. Before she could catch her breath, he'd grasped her arms and drawn her up to him, his mouth hot near hers. "Tender, huh? That's the way you want it?"

Something flared in his eyes, something beautiful. It was the very tenderness he spoke of, and it made him look like an angel of darkness. Bev waited for his mouth to come down on hers. She was already dizzy with the heat and the smell and the sight of him. He was so powerful in the way he took control, so sure of himself in everything he did that it overwhelmed her fragile grip on reality. He knew what he wanted, but she didn't know anything except the sensations that streamed through her every time he touched her this way.

His grip on her arms was bruising, but his mouth was soft as he touched it to a corner of her lips. "I can be tender, babe. I can be anything you want."

Some sweet emotion surged inside Bev at his husky avowal. She couldn't put a name to the sudden poignancy that burned her throat and pressed down on her heart, but it drove her nearly crazy with the need to be close to him. "Then show me," she said, her voice breaking. "Show me how tender you can be."

He sought her face with his hands, a hint of unsteadiness in his rigid fingers. He wanted to be gentle, she could feel it. But the ache was in him too. He was fighting a rage of desire.

The next touch of his mouth was fever-sweet and searching. It pulled up a sensation from deep within her, a soft cry of longing. She needed to be in his arms. She needed him close, closer. "Wait," she said, pressing her fingers to his lips. "Wait, please . . ."

She swung around to face him, letting her skirt hike up. "Remember how this worked?"

His eyes said he couldn't believe what she was doing. "Yes, I remember."

"Tender," she pleaded as he moved between her legs. His eyes flared again, beautifully, as he stared at her.

He nudged open her aching legs with his powerful thighs, inching her skirt farther up, exposing flushed, vibrant skin. Her stomach muscles pulled tight when he came up against her.

"Yes, I remember," he said, dragging her closer, his hands on her hips.

She wore only silk panties, and she felt every steel inch of him as he moved against her softness. She had never felt more vulnerable to a man in her life. Pleasure speared through her, impaling her as she allowed herself to imagine what he would do next, and the dizzying rapture it would bring her.

She resisted his kiss for a second, just for the giddy pleasure of giving in. A sigh flowed through her like water as she opened to the melting warmth of his mouth, to the deep sword-thrust of his tongue. The kiss wasn't tender, as he'd promised. It was harsh and sweet and hungry, but it thrilled her soul.

His mouth moved over hers and she felt the scar that snaked down from his lower lip. She drew back, curious, needing to look at him, expecting to see the tenderness again. "I want to touch you," she said impulsively, running her fingers along his lips. "You really are a beautiful man"—her voice went soft as she traced the jagged line—"in so many ways. Maybe you do have the soul of a poet, just as Arthur said."

It was the wrong thing to say to Sam Nichols. He drew back and caught her face in his hands, his thumbs working at the soft flesh of her cheeks. "Beautiful?" he repeated, his voice husky with disbelief. "Poet? What are you talking about? You've got me confused with somebody else."

"No! I just meant that you're more than you seem. You're—" She stopped, afraid she was making it worse.

He searched her face as though she weren't making any sense, as though her attempt to compliment him was somehow suspect. "I'm exactly what I seem. Maybe you need to get that straight. And what the hell does Arthur have to do with this?"

Bev saw the extent of her mistake then. Sam was a powder keg. He was torn with jealousy, but he couldn't admit it, just as he couldn't admit his own vulnerability. It was second nature for a man like him to question motives, to mistrust even a kind gesture.

She was trying to decide if there was any safe way to explain herself to him, when she heard a knock at the cabin door. A rustle of sound drew her attention to an envelope being slipped under the door. "Look," she whispered.

Sam went to pick it up. Kneeling, he ripped open the envelope, read the note, and crushed it in his hand. "Your lunch date, lovely creature. You're late."

Bev hurried up the stairway, smoothing her dress as she rushed to join Arthur for lunch. Her legs felt wobbly and she was still trembling from the encounter with Sam. She had to get herself calmed down.

As she dashed out onto the Promenade Deck, a fine mist sheened her skin. She glanced up at the spindrift of clouds overhead and smiled. They looked like white powder puffs arranged on a rich, velvet-blue swath of sky. The mist was one of the sun showers the tropics were known for, she realized. She'd been told it wasn't unusual for them to occur several times a day. A lone cloud would whoosh in, dump its warm, steamy load, and whoosh away.

Impulsively, she held up her face to the delicate veil of moisture. She was still a little flushed and feverish, and the tepid rain felt marvelous. She closed her eyes a moment and absently ran her fingers over the dampness collecting on her lips and down her arched throat. Soft, startled laughter welled up, warming her breath. What was happening to her? Was she becoming a pleasure seeker?

"Hey, gorgeous!"

The shouted greeting startled Bev out of her reverie. Tony, the man she'd mistaken for Arthur, was jogging down the deck toward her, a gold St. Christopher's medal bobbing against his tanned, hairless chest. He wasn't a bad-looking man, she admitted, but definitely not her type.

"Where you been hiding, lover?" he said, jogging in place. "I've been searching this banana boat for you since the bon voyage party. You never gave me your last name."

"Actually, I was just on my way somewhere." She began to walk toward the restaurant, wondering how she was going to get rid of Tony. Had she ever been in this situation before? Leaving a torrid encounter with one man, then trying to get rid of a second so she could meet a third?

He jogged alongside her. "Hey, no problem, babe. I'll walk you there."

Now she had two of them calling her babe. That couldn't be a good omen. "I have plans, Tony."

She glanced around, looking for a way to escape, and saw her dance partner coming directly toward her. Unfortunately, he saw her too. A fireplug of a man, he spread his arms wide in welcome.

"Shake your booty!" he sang out.

Bev smiled wanly. *Four* men in her heretofore manless life. Was this an embarrassment of riches, or what. "Later, maybe?" she said as her dance partner shimmied up.

The man Bev didn't notice in her "embarrassment of riches" was a shadowy figure who was watching the entire episode from the cover of a lifeboat bow. Sam Nichols could have saved Bev from her surplus of suitors, but he'd decided to let her sweat it out. His conscience was back at it, nagging him again, but he was taking great pleasure in ignoring it. Served her right, he told himself . . . dressing like a Barbie doll, dancing like a harem girl, throwing her head back in the rain. She was giving off enough body language to attract sperm whales.

"Bev!"

Sam looked up to see Arthur on the deck above calling down to her. He held up a single red rose as he started down the stairway. Bev immediately excused herself, leaving her puzzled admirers in the dust as she rushed to meet Blankenship. Sam had never seen two poor suckers get the gate so quickly.

"You dear, sweet man," she said, pressing a quick kiss to Arthur's cheek as she took the rose from him.

Blankenship looked as if he were about to faint. Sam turned away in disgust. This was getting sickening, he decided. He wanted to stalk off and let the two of them wallow in mushy romantic swill. But the truth was, his stomach was tying itself up in queasy little knots. Even his breathing was off, quick and harsh. Motion sickness, he told himself, glaring out at the vast expanse of bright, rolling water. It had to be that.

Sam hunkered down over the railing, pretending to be admiring the view as Bev and Arthur passed. They were so busy laughing and hanging on to each other's arms, he doubted they would have noticed if he'd jumped overboard. He could feel heat pooling at the base of his neck as they disappeared from sight. What he needed was a good, long swim in an ice-cold pool.

He headed for the cabin to change, and by the time he reached it, he'd decided the only changes that were in order were between himself and Ms. Brewster. She'd accused him of jealousy, and that was exactly how he was acting—like a brainless idiot. It was damn embarrassing.

He made no further attempt to analyze the situation beyond assuring himself that he could easily get things under control with some judicious exercising of his willpower. After all, he had no interest in Bev Brewster other than the obvious sexual thing. He'd never been jealous of a woman in his life, and he wasn't going to start now. Dueling at dawn wasn't his style.

It had to be the physical attraction making him crazy. He'd let himself get turned on so high, it had burnt out his neural circuits. He couldn't think straight, he wasn't sleeping right. Just last night he'd lain awake, staring at the ceiling, wishing he could tie one on and drink himself into a stupor.

The solution was obvious. He had to keep his hands off her. It was better that way anyway. There was Harve to think about, there was the case, and there was his own sanity. From now on, Nichols, he told himself, you're going to keep your nose clean, your fly buttoned, and your hands to yourself.

He stripped off his T-shirt and flung it across the room, triumphant, the captain of his soul once more. B. J. Brewster could dance naked in front of him, she could drop to her knees and beg, and he still wouldn't touch her.

Eight

Bev should have been having the time of her life. The first few days of the cruise sailed by in a giddy whirl of masquerade balls, glittering stage shows, calypso music, and limbo dancing. She was undeniably the belle of the ship, but nothing in her background had prepared her for such extravagant amounts of male attention. Arthur doted on her. Tony flirted with her every chance he got. Her dance partner, whose name turned out to be Sergio, was married, but that didn't stop him from tossing her playful winks and shaking his shoulders.

She didn't know whether to blame it on the cruise, on Arthur and her retinue of male admirers, or on Sam Nichols, but she'd changed dramatically from the woman who was afraid to leave the safety of her Encino home. Now Bev Brewster laughed and danced and boogied with the best of them. She struck up conversations and returned smiles. She juggled coconuts in the Passenger Talent Show.

She wasn't sure if she liked the new Bev, or if the changes would hold once she'd returned to California. In her more fanciful moods she wondered if the Caribbean sun showers were a form of magic dust and they were all on a strange, enchanted voyage.

There was only one thing she'd become reasonably

certain of in the last week, and that concerned Sam. He wasn't himself. He was behaving strangely, to say the least. He hadn't touched her since their showdown in the cabin. He wouldn't talk to her except to discuss business, and then he was terse and remote. He slept on the floor without even flipping to see who got the bed.

And now, at two in the morning, as she lay sleepless on the bunk, listening to the heavy drone of the engine, she fought the urge to roll to her side and call his name. He'd been restless all night, tossing and turning, letting out little groans in his sleep. Once he'd said something unintelligible and she had whimsically decided it was the nickname he'd given her, Lace.

"Sam," she whispered, "are you awake? I want to talk to you about the case, okay?"

She heard a heavy sigh as he rolled to his back, opened his eyes, and stared up at the ceiling. "What about the case?"

"Arthur's not taking the bait," she said, thinking quickly. She hadn't actually expected Sam to respond.

"Surely you jest. The fish is hooked and landed. You could grill him for dinner."

Bev tried to decide if it was sarcasm or rampant boredom she heard in Sam's voice. Some choice, she thought. "I meant the financial bait. I let it slip that I'd come into a great deal of money recently, but he wasn't even interested enough to ask me how much. Isn't he supposed to be trying to talk me into a phony investment deal?"

"He will," Sam said, turning his back to her again. "Ask him for some investment advice. He'll bite."

"You're sure?" In her heart of hearts she almost hoped Arthur wouldn't bite. Perhaps Sam was right, and she had lost her professional objectivity, but she had trouble imagining Arthur taking advantage of anyone.

When Sam didn't answer, she released a sigh and rolled to her back, gazing up at the ceiling. This wasn't going well. Perhaps she ought to be grateful that Sam had backed off, but she wasn't. His remoteness made her feel strangely bereft, as thought he'd already become a part of her life, a touchstone of sorts. Some kind of emotional bonding had taken place, she realized, at least on her part. That seemed impossible with a man as difficult and inaccessible as he was, but he had stirred feelings and needs. . . .

Most of them were sexual, she admitted, aware of the soft ache in her loins that wouldn't go away. She actually missed him. She drew up her legs as a jolt of longing rocked through her. Lord, she did. She missed the rough thrill of his touch, the power, even the crudeness. What did that mean?

She closed her eyes, unwilling to try to analyze the confusing relationship. She just wanted him talking to her again, that was all, even sarcastically. She wanted him to acknowledge that she was there, alive.

Sam knew she was alive. He was aware of every breath she took, every whisper of the sheets beneath her body, every rustle of her sable hair against the pillow. He'd kept his vow. He'd stayed away from her, but it hadn't eased his turmoil any. Much as he hated to admit it, seeing her with other men was driving him nuts. Sleeping in this cabin with her was driving him nuts. He woke up in pain night after night, as hard as the floor he slept on. Tonight he'd come awake with her name on his lips, and with a tightness around his heart that wouldn't let him breathe. If there was a limit to how much a man could take, he'd hit it. Days ago!

"You've never crushed passion plums with your bare feet?" Arthur pretended shock. "Well, now's your chance." He pushed back from their table for two, raising his voice to be heard over the din of the party crowd. "Let's do it!"

"Oh, Arthur . . ." Bev considered the huge wooden vat of purple fruit and the couples frolicking inside it, pants rolled up, skirts held high. The island they'd docked at that morning produced a sparkling wine made from the exotic fruit, and according to West Indian folklore, the juice of the passion plum had aphrodisiacal properties. The entire cruise ship had been invited to attend the annual winemaking festival, but Bev wasn't in the mood for revelry.

"I don't think so," she said as Arthur leaned close and draped an arm around her waist.

"Is something wrong? You haven't touched your drink."

"I'm fine," she assured him quickly, smiling. She picked up her wineglass, took a sip, and nodded her appreciation. "Delicious, really. I wouldn't have missed this for anything."

Arthur beamed, happy once more.

Lighten up, Bev, she told herself. *At least you could look as though you're having a good time.* Her pensive mood was certain to provoke Arthur's curiosity eventually, and she didn't want him quizzing her about her personal problems.

She sipped the wine and pretended to be fascinated by the entertainment, which really was marvelous. Stilt dancers, fire eaters, and sword throwers delighted the crowd with their exotic and dangerous feats. Fiery torches burned high in the velvet darkness, and sensual music thrummed, penetrating the senses as vibrantly as the wine.

It was a fabulous party, and one Bev might have enjoyed thoroughly if she hadn't been so distracted. She glanced around the crowd, looking for Sam. She hadn't seen him since he'd stumbled into the cabin at three that morning, obviously under the influence. She'd tried to talk to him, but he'd rebuffed her, making some vague reference about women holding the ace hand. When she'd kept after him, trying to learn what was wrong, he'd walked out without telling her where he was going.

"More wine, lovely lady?"

Bev glanced up as Arthur refilled her glass. He set the carafe down and gazed at her, his head tilting like a child's as he searched her features. There was obvious concern in his eyes.

"What's wrong, Bev? Is it me? Have I done something?"

"You? No! Oh, Arthur, of course not. You're wonderful company. I'm enjoying myself, really. Here," she said, raising her wineglass. "Let's toast to a good time."

They clinked glasses and Bev drank deeply. She had to get Sam Nichols off her mind. He was distracting her from her job, which was to establish a relationship with Arthur. He was also ruining a perfectly good party without even being at it.

"By the way, I just finished the book you loaned me," she told Arthur, leaning toward him as though she intended to share something personal and confidential. "It was wonderful."

Arthur's eyes lit up. "You liked it too?"

A moment later they were huddling together, discussing passages in the book and comparing the differing philosophies of the two poets, Byron and Shelley. Arthur expounded on Shelley's idealism at length, but Bev preferred Byron's more jaded, satirical view of the world. As they laughed and talked, Arthur continued to refill their glasses. And Bev continued to sip.

The wine was delicious, she decided, wondering how many glasses she'd had. It was light-bodied, piquantly sweet, and redolent with the heady perfume of passion plums. She could easily have drunk the whole carafe herself if she hadn't been warned not to imbibe freely while wearing a seasick patch.

"Seasick patch!" She sat up and touched the bandage on her neck. "You're not supposed to drink with these things!"

Arthur grinned and splashed some more wine into her glass. "You're not on a ship now. Why don't you take it off?"

"Arthur," Bev said, pretending to be scandalized.

"Dah dah dum, dah-dah dah dum." Arthur hummed the bump-and-grind stripper's anthem, winking at her mischievously. He was obviously a little high, and Bev was beginning to feel the effects of the wine herself. Warmth was spreading up the back of her neck, and her earlobes were tingling.

"Here goes," she said, rolling her shoulder as she peeled off the bandage. She ticked the patch back and forth as though she'd just removed a long black glove, and then she tossed it into the crowd.

Arthur convulsed in giggles as the bandage stuck to her fingers. "Goodness," he said breathlessly, "I'm getting squiffy. How about you? Maybe we should dance it off?"

"What a brilliant idea!"

Bev felt a little squiffy herself as she and Arthur undulated to the sensual reggae rhythms. Her face was flushed with color, and the music pulsed around her irresistibly, as though it were daring her to let go of her concerns and give in to the festive mood. Her peasant blouse kept slipping off her shoulders as she danced, and for some reason that struck Arthur as enchantingly funny. He fought off one hit of giggles after another, and his efforts were so sweetly hilarious that Bev finally lost control too.

Arthur tried to take her in his arms as the music turned slow, but neither of them could dance worth a darn. Instead, they held on to each other helplessly, laughing, swaying. It was a good thing Sam hadn't shown up, Bev decided as she wrapped her arms around Arthur's neck. He wouldn't like her having so much fun.

Bev didn't know the half of it. Sam *was* there. He was posted not fifty feet from her, watching her every tipsy move. He'd been there the entire night, hidden in the shadows of the bandstand, a forbidding presence in his street uniform—jeans, T-shirt, and black leather jacket. One look at him, and Bev would have sobered up quickly. He was as silent and ominous as unexploded nitroglycerin.

Sam Nichols was having a bad night. He was fighting

off a massive hangover, the urge to do serious bodily harm, *and* the annoying racket of his conscience, which was trying to tell him he had no business judging Bev for her behavior when he'd just tied one on the night before. His conscience was losing the battle.

Sam was a muscle twitch away from breaking up the whole damn party. One twitch. He didn't like the way every male in the place was ogling Bev, including the ship's captain. He didn't like the way Arthur's hands were glued to her swiveling hips, and he damn sure didn't like the way she had draped herself on Arthur's neck. If she didn't settle down and start behaving herself, the winemaking festival was going up in flames.

Even the dress she had on made his head throb. It was one of those peasant jobbies with big flowers and flounces that hung off her shoulders and looked as though it was going to drop to the ground any second. She couldn't be wearing a bra underneath the way she was jiggling, and if she guzzled any more wine, she was going to get totally swacked.

Swacked, he thought, not a half-bad idea. A primitive fantasy flashed through his tortured brain, and a grim smile surfaced, the first in days. His jaw clenched tighter as he pictured himself throwing her over his shoulder, hauling her off, and teaching her a thing or two about standard operating procedure. Spanking a fully grown woman as an object lesson was as obsolete as the horse-drawn carriage, but he didn't give a damn about social history at the moment. He was so far gone, even his personal aversion to that kind of practice didn't faze him. The fantasy brought him almost as much perverse satisfaction as the one where he drowned Arthur by dragging him behind the ship on a bowline.

He let the imagined scene roll through his mind again, slowly, detail for detail, until a little shriek of laughter brought him back to reality. By the time he looked up, Bev and Arthur were bouncing around in the vat of plums, Bev holding her skirts high and cavorting like an island nymph.

Sam's self-control was already stretched past the breaking point when Bev's dress slipped off her shoulder, nearly exposing a breast. Arthur let out a delighted gasp and tried to shield her as he pulled the material back up. Bev giggled and swiped at his marauding hands.

Sam saw red. Arthur may have been trying to help, but to Sam it looked like nothing more than a cheap excuse to fondle a woman's breasts. He reached the wooden vat on a dead run, vaulting over the side, boots and all. "Back off, lover boy," he said, shoving Arthur aside. The smaller man went down, disappearing in the purple glop.

"That man's got his shoes on!" a woman screeched.

"Who is he?" another cried. "What's he doing in here?"

"Sam?" Bev said, belatedly aware of his presence. She'd been trying to rescue Arthur, who couldn't seem to stay on his feet. She turned unsteadily, abandoning Arthur to the glop. "When did you get here, Sam?"

"The party's over, Lace." Sam grabbed her hand and pulled her with him to the side of the vat. "You're coming with me."

"I think I'm going to be sick," Bev mumbled as Sam strode up the gangplank of the cruise ship. She was unceremoniously draped over his shoulder and swinging like a bag of dirty laundry as the world floated by her, upside down. She knew she ought to be kicking and screaming and doing all the things abducted women did in the movies, but she didn't have the stomach for it. Literally.

Nearly all the passengers and ship's brass were at the festival, which left only a few waiters and crew members to gape as Sam ferried her through the ship's narrow corridors.

"Put me down," Bev whispered. "Everybody's looking."

"Let 'em look."

"Why are you carrying me?" she demanded to know.

"Because you're bombed on your butt."

"My what? Where are we going?"

"The cabin," Sam muttered. "And a nice cold shower."

"Shower? No!"

Sam paid no attention to her halfhearted protest. Once they were in the cabin, he propped her up against the shower stall as he reached inside and turned the water on. "Get your clothes off," he said. "You're a sorry-looking mess."

"Am not." Bev glanced down dizzily at her magenta feet and legs, and then, with effort, she looked back up at Sam, trying to bring him into focus. He was fruit-splattered and demon-eyed, but there was the cutest little red blotch on his nose, a semi-crushed bit of passion plum. "Don't look any worse than you do."

"Ditch the island-nymph ensemble," he said, "unless you want me to do it for you."

She shook her head—and nearly lost her balance.

Exhaling a curse, Sam reluctantly grabbed a handful of her peasant blouse by its loose elastic neckline and dragged it down her torso, letting it lay in a pile at her feet. He stripped off her skirt next, leaving her standing there in nothing but her panties, her clothing a colorful pool at her feet.

Bev stared at her naked breasts, one plum-stained, one not. "How did that happen?" she asked absently.

Sam's stomach fisted at the sight of her nearly nude body. She didn't seem to be aware that he'd undressed her, and oddly, her nonchalance made her that much more irresistible. He wanted to touch her so badly, his teeth ached.

"Let's get you cleaned up," he said, turning her around and herding her into the shower. The sooner he got this object lesson over with, the better, he'd decided. There was no reasoning with a soused, half-naked woman. He'd get her sobered up and then he'd give her holy hell.

He no sooner had her in the shower with the door

shut when she bounced back out again, dripping. "All done," she chirped.

"Like hell. Get back in there."

She shook her head, water flying in every direction.

"In that case, I'm coming in with you." Sam pulled off his shirt and boots and pushed her back into the stall, crowding in behind her. The spray soaked them both instantly. "You're not getting out of here until you can say your name backward."

She began trying immediately. Before she was through, Sam had heard so many garbled versions of Beverly Jean, he wished he'd never brought it up.

"Veb?" she said finally, twisting around to grin at him.

"Enough chitchat," Sam muttered.

It was a tight fit in the tiny shower stall, very tight. Bev insisted on wriggling around to face him, and the soft, wet squish of her breasts against his bare chest was enough to give Sam a serious muscle spasm in a vulnerable place. She was making him crazy, and what was worse, she didn't seem to know it.

He whipped the cold knob on full force, but the closest he could get to an icy, sobering shower was a lukewarm spray. He held her under it anyway, letting the water run over her face and stream down her shoulders and chest. The sight of her wet and glistening breasts sent a lightning bolt of desire through him. Tension burned deep in the pit of his gut, flaring all the way to the soles of his feet.

"How are we doing?" he said, holding Bev back so he could inspect her.

"Who wants to know?" She smiled at him dreamily, as though she were thoroughly enjoying his dilemma, to whatever extent she was aware of it. Maybe instead of spanking her, he would dump her over the side and drag her behind the boat with Arthur. Maybe he'd do both!

In fact, Bev *was* enjoying herself. The world had stopped swinging, her stomach was pretty well settled, and she was thoroughly drenched with warm, sexy water. Even Sam seemed a little less edgy, or so her slightly foggy brain concluded from the fact that he'd joined her in the shower. She wasn't exactly sure what he was doing in there with her, but it felt kind of pleasant pressed up against him. She hadn't been this close to him in so long.

"You have a very nice chest," she said. There were other things about him she could have mentioned, but she happened to be staring directly at his chest, and the streaming water was making fascinating patterns in his dark hair. He did have the most beautiful body hair.

"Thank you." He smiled faintly. "Yours is nice too."

"My chest?" She met his eyes and saw the fierce, dazzling blue they had become. The scar that drew at his mouth was nearly white from the tension in his jaw. Something about the way he looked made her strain a little harder to breathe, as though the steam in their tiny shower stall had absorbed all the oxygen. Her legs ached a little too, with that sweet, pulling sensation she'd come to associate with him.

A fanciful notion filled her head as she vaguely remembered how he'd dragged her out of the vat and thrown her over his shoulder. He could have been a ruthless Caribbean pirate, the decadent, bodice-ripping type who regularly abducted women for their own pleasure. He certainly looked ferocious enough. But wouldn't a pirate be ravishing her by now? The possibility might have alarmed her if it hadn't been for the soothing water. She felt as though her insides were streaming with warmth, smooth and silvery, everything gone to liquid. She didn't have a muscle or a bone in her body.

"Don't you just love showers?" she said, letting her head loll back and the water run over her face.

"Careful," he said, catching hold of her.

His hands slid down her back, one of them ending up very near her derriere. The sudden feel of him there sent an erotic lightning bolt through Bev. It was a sensation as sharp and bitingly sweet as the snap of leather recoiling in the air. She'd never felt anything so riveting.

"What are you doing?" she asked softly, a gasp in her voice.

"Keeping you on your feet. We don't want an accident in the shower, do we?"

"No. No accidents." Suddenly aware of him in a very different way, she couldn't take her eyes off him. Details leaped out at her with dizzying clarity. The flare of his nostrils when he breathed, the aggressive bones of his face overlaid by fine-grained tawny skin. Had he always been so tall, and broad at the shoulders? He seemed to be touching the shower stall on both sides. She felt surrounded by him, completely engulfed.

He moved against her, and she felt the heaviness of wet denim abrading her bare skin. "Do you know you have your jeans on?" she asked.

He smiled, his eyes darkening. "I think the party girl is finally sobering up."

No, Bev wasn't sober, not by a long shot. She was simply aware. Suddenly, painfully aware of him, of herself, and of the sensual signals coursing riotously through her body. She could feel him through the wet denim. He was hard against her, huge against her. The constant thrumming pressure on her pelvic bone set off an explosion of excitement deep in her belly. She felt dizzy and drunk again. Dizzy with sensation, drunk with wanting to see and touch what was underneath the denim.

"Couldn't be very comfortable," she said, looking up at him. "Wet jeans."

"Not comfortable," he agreed, "but safe."

Their eyes met, and Bev fell silent. He knew, she realized. He knew she was tingling with curiosity and excitement. Burning. It was as though he'd been eavesdropping on her thoughts.

"If the jeans bother you . . ." he said.

"You could take them off," she suggested.

His voice got husky. "Or you could."

Bev's heart went wild as he reached for her hand and drew it to the button fly of his jeans.

It occurred to her that she ought to protest, but she was driven by curiosity. She moved her fingers gingerly, each new discovery sending another lightning bolt through her. When she finally found the top button, it was slick and stubborn, refusing to cooperate as she tried to force it through the shrunken opening. "I can't," she said, frustration surging in her voice.

He took over, silently freeing each button.

He wore no underwear.

Bev's breathing deepened, growing slow as he brought her hand back. She touched him, and a shock wave of sensation ripped through her hand. He was rigid and hot to the touch, like steel and silk about to burst into flames. She curled her hand around him, forgetting to be frightened, and he let out a sound that was as racked with anguish as it was ecstasy.

"I'm sorry," she said softly, knowing she hadn't hurt him. She was giving him more pleasure than he could bear. Her fingers curved instinctively to the shape of him.

"Enough," he pleaded. But she couldn't stop. Touching him thrilled her. It filled her with a harsh, nameless yearning that clutched at her vitals.

Looking at him, she waited, and when he opened his eyes, there was something incredulous there, something touched by wonder. She squeezed her hand and watched the lights flare in his irises. The blue turned a deep, roaring indigo, an inferno of carnal urges and animal desires. She'd never seen anything so beautiful.

Without a thought to the consequences, she knelt and brought him to her lips, tasting the wetness, the hardness. Her mouth softened against burning steel, and a current of electricity stroked her feminine parts, so powerful she could hardly move. Her legs felt weak and useless, stunned by the force. Her heart was a deep throb that pulsed in her swollen lips. She closed her eyes, surrendering to the pulse for several seconds. The urges clamoring inside her were too frenetic to understand or satisfy, except one. She felt an overpowering impulse to take him into her mouth, deeply, completely. She wanted to consume him, but she was too weak with paralyzing excitement.

"Help me," she whimpered.

"Help you?" A profanity shook on his lips. He caught hold of her arm and tore her hand away from him, dragging her up to his mouth. His hands bit into the flesh of her arms as he brought her to her tiptoes, nearly lifting her off the floor. His kiss was harsh and brutal and consuming. It punished her for the sweet pain she brought him. It promised her savage pleasure.

Sam had no conscious thought of punishing her. The forces inside him were too primal for conscious control. He was mindless with need. He had to get inside her, to know how deep she could take him, to feel her squeezing him the way her hand had. There was no other way to survive the maelstrom his body had become.

"I'm going to help you, babe," he said, lodging her up against the shower wall. "I'm going to help us both."

She breathed an anguished plea as he stripped off her soaked panties and brought up her leg. The urge to enter her immediately slammed through him like a fist. He wanted to take her right then, rough and quick, no preliminaries, but he controlled the impulse.

He tasted her mouth, drinking the beads of warm water that caught on her upper lip. She was soft and hot and open to him. And she was hungry, he could tell by the way she dug her nails into his biceps when he stroked the inner silk of her raised thigh. Her soft gasps of pleasure nearly drove him crazy, but he held back, stroking nearer and nearer the source of her excitement.

"Like this?" he said, swirling his fingers up to the place where her soft brown hair curled wildly. "Do you like being touched like this?" He combed his fingers into the vibrant thatch.

Her head fell back helplessly, and then she stiffened, arching against him as he cupped the mound between her legs with his palm. "Yes," she breathed, hardly able to speak. "Yes, there . . . touch me there, please . . . harder."

"Harder?" He knew exactly what she wanted, but he couldn't bring himself to give it to her so quickly. He was in the throes of a sensation so sweet it made him want to groan. He had to make it last. "And here too?" he said, delving into her warm folds with his fingers and using his thumb to encircle the part of her that was swollen with desire.

She couldn't speak. She could only nod her head.

He stroked her gently, mercilessly, letting her move against his hand until the mounting pain of his own desire forced him to act. He probed deeper, slipping a finger inside her as she cried out with choked rapture. She was hot and wet, muscles as taut as her demon fingers had been. Her throbbing warmth told him everything he needed to know. She wanted him inside her as much as he wanted to be there.

He withdrew and pressed her to the wall, straining to hold her still.

"Easy, Lace," he said, unable to subdue her frantic movements long enough to enter her. The aching throb between his legs became unbearable, and he gripped her by the arms, lifting her over him, bringing her down. A knifelike sensation pierced his groin as he found what he was seeking. Her lush warmth yielded to his muscular thrusts, and he entered her with a passion that was primal.

Once he was truly, deeply inside her, once that barrier of flesh and will had been crossed, he lost control to the urgent demands of his body. He kissed her ravenously, running his hands over her nakedness, cupping her breasts and buttocks roughly, tenderly. She clung to him, gasping as he impaled her, nailing her sweet, undulating body to the wall.

Bev felt as though she were being rocked and jolted

with ecstasy. A deep, radiating pleasure gripped her, pulling irresistibly at her muscles. It seemed to peak with his thrusts, to caress every shimmering nerve. She locked her arms around his powerful neck, vowing never to let him go. There was an urgent need flowering inside her. She wanted to be crushed in his arms, pinned by his weight. She wanted him to open her legs and mount her in the way that men and woman had been making love since the beginning of time.

She wanted to feel like a woman again. She needed that so desperately. But when she tried to tell him, the words were breathless and nearly incomprehensible. "Please . . . carry me to the bed," was all she could say.

She refused to let him pull out. Instead, she wrapped her arms around his neck and curled herself to him as he shouldered open the shower door. A billowy cloud of steam escaped with them as he carried her to the bed. Bev felt him plunging even more deeply with every step, and then they fell onto the flowered bedspread, still joined, rolling and flashing and thrusting until somehow they ended up with him on his back.

Bev gave out a cry of shocked satisfaction and arched above him. "Wait a minute," he rasped, cupping her breasts as she began to flex slowly, throwing her head back, moving up and down on him, heedless of the utter wantonness of her movements. "How did we end up like this?"

"Just lucky—" She barely got the words out before new and sharper heights of sensation took her. Every minute move she made, even the tiniest twitch of her muscles, brought the most unbearable ecstasy. "No, it's too much," she said, her voice choked with startled disbelief. "I won't survive this."

She shuddered and stopped, unable to move, her legs weighted and throbbing.

Sam's body screamed in protest. Muscles seized in his gut and his thighs. "We're not stopping now, babe." He hauled her into his arms and rolled her onto her back. "Not now." He was racked with the need to hold her, to make love to her—rough, tender, whatever she wanted. He'd never felt anything so powerful before.

"No, don't ever stop, Sam," she said, a strange, sweet urgency in her voice. "Make love to me. Do it all to me. Everything. Every sexy, incredible thing a man and woman can do."

Her eyes glittered and danced like stars reflected on water. There was a wildness in them that blew Sam's mind. Was it the wine talking? Or the woman? His conscience tried to tell him that she might not know what she was doing, but he was too bewitched by her sensuality, too crazy with desire to pay it any heed. If she wanted him to romp naked through the cruise ship and swing on chandeliers with her, he would do it.

Nine

Bev woke up to a frantic tapping on the cabin door. At first she thought she was in her small Encino bedroom and Southern California was having another earthquake. Why else would the house be rumbling and vibrating? As she rolled her head and saw the naked man sprawled on his stomach, his arms thrown wide, his head partially covered by a pillow, she knew she was a very long way from Encino.

She sat up gingerly, trying to remember why she was in bed with a naked man, but her forehead was throbbing just above her left eye, and she couldn't concentrate on details. Also, someone was calling her name.

"Bev! Are you in there?"

"Who is it?" she asked, wincing at the sound of her own voice.

" It's me, Arthur," the voice called. "Are you all right?"

Arthur? She touched her forehead. Who did she know named Arthur?

"Bev, it's me," he said again. "Everything happened so fast, I didn't know what hit me. By the time they got me out of the wine vat, you were gone."

Wine vat, Arthur . . . Arthur, wine vat. What was happening to her memory? She vaguely recalled a warning about memory disturbances on the box her seasick patches came in. She'd removed the patch, but if the drug was still in her system—

"The way you disappeared, I was afraid you were angry with me," he said. "I didn't mean to touch your breast, Bev. That was an accident."

Touch her breast? Oh, of course, Arthur. It was coming back to her now, in little bits and pieces of detail, in large chunks. She'd been at a party with Arthur, crushing passion plums with her bare feet and—

She glanced down at her own undeniably nude body, at the wet shambles of a bed where she and Sam were sprawled, at the room with its, soggy, plum-stained clothes thrown every which way, and let out a tiny moan of despair. Was that water dripping off the ceiling? It looked as though they'd had an orgy. Her moan degenerated into a husky groan. It looked as though they'd turned her tiny cabin into the Roman baths.

"Bev! Are you in there! Are you all right?"

She struggled off the bed, dragging a blanket with her as far as it would go, which wasn't far enough. An edge of the material caught beneath Sam's dead weight, and she couldn't budge it.

"Bev?"

"I'm fine, Arthur," she whispered, darting to the door, naked and shivering. "I was feeling a little lightheaded, so I came back to the ship."

"What did you say, Bev? I can hardly hear you."

She cupped her hand to the door and whispered louder. "It's very late, Arthur, and I'm a little under the weather at the moment." Somehow she had to get rid of him without waking up Sam. She needed some time to figure out what had gone on in this dripping room.

"How about breakfast in the morning?" she suggested. "No, make that lunch. Does lunch sound good?"

It took a little more whispering and wheedling, but she finally got Arthur to leave. Breathing a sigh of relief, she turned around to find Sam propped up on his elbow, looking like an indolent Greek god as he surveyed the situation. A smile tugged at his handsome mouth, and Bev came face-to-face with one of life's immutable truths: There wasn't any way to adequately cover the naked female body with only two hands.

"Stop staring at me," she said sharply. "I'm naked."

"I noticed." His voice was wry, husky, a man mightily pleased with his circumstances. "You were naked the last time I looked too."

"Either turn the other way, or close your eyes."

"You're no fun."

The bedspread was in a heap on the floor, and Bev made a dash for it as he averted his eyes. "What do you mean, the last time you looked?" she said, wrapping herself like a mummy in the fabric's jungle motif.

"Well, you weren't naked the entire time," he conceded. "You had your panties on in the shower—for a while."

"Shower?" More details were creeping back into Bev's head, strange and lurid flashes she would have preferred not to remember. Perhaps she'd had a terrible dream while she was asleep. "I took a shower? Why did I do that?"

"You were a mess, babe, plum wine head to toe, but we got you cleaned up pretty good."

"We?" Bev felt an immediate clutch of anxiety. She searched through her memory as though she were in a darkroom processing negatives—until she came to a slide show that astonished her. She saw herself naked and arched over a man as if they were doing something unbelievably sensual. She saw herself moving above him, touching and caressing him as if she were the aggressor. No . . . impossible!

But her mind flashed slide after slide, as though determined to convince her that she'd made wild, abandoned love with him, that she'd flung herself on top of his beautiful, battle-scarred body and ravished him.

"Did something happen in this room?" she asked Sam breathlessly. "Besides the shower?"

"Something?" The smile that glowed through his

dark features made his eyes smoky and dangerously intimate. "You're not even close, Lace. It was more like everything."

"I don't believe you." She clutched the towel to her breasts and shook her head, alarmed by his raffish grin. "All right, then," she demanded. "Just what did we do? Tell me."

"You don't remember anything?"

She stepped back, refusing to commit herself. She remembered some things, all right, she just didn't want to believe what she remembered. The details were still sketchy. Damn that seasick patch anyway. She ought to have paid more attention to the warning label. The plum wine hadn't helped either. "We took a shower, right? I remember that, and then—"

His smile widened, implying the worst.

"What are you saying?" she bristled. "That we did something wrong? Something . . . indecent?"

"I thought it was damn decent. You don't remember? Not even being on top?" He sighed. "It was your idea, Lace."

"Me? On top? Of you? No, I didn't do that, I wasn't—" She stopped babbling, caught her breath, and glared at him. She hadn't been dreaming. No such luck. "You're saying we made love, I was on top, and it was *my* idea?"

"Hey, that was just the first time."

Her voice dropped off. "The first time?"

"Oh, babe—" He broke off, laughing softly, as though he could hardly contain the images crowding his brain.

Bev caught at her upper lip with her teeth. What *had* they done? She could see that he fully intended to leave her with the impression that they had committed myriad and unspeakable acts. She did sort of remember the being-on-top part. Actually, she was beginning to recall some astonishing things . . . arching over him, bouncing up and down, throwing her head back and laughing like some pagan priestess during spring fertility rites.

She pressed two fingers to her throbbing eyebrow.

This was looking very bad. If she'd done those things, what else had she done? A hint of desperation sneaked into her voice as she glanced at Sam. "You should be ashamed of yourself," she said.

"Me?"

"Yes, I was high on those damn fermented plums. I didn't know what I was doing."

"Oh, right, likely excuse."

"Can't you even be a gentleman about it?"

He fixed her with a long, penetrating look that said it was too late for polite pretenses. "Now she wants me to be a gentleman?" he said softly. "Is this the same woman who whispered in my ear 'Make me scream for mercy, Sam'?"

"I did not!" she gasped.

His eyes implied that she had whispered that and more. Shame and disbelief flooded her face with stinging heat. She couldn't have said such a revolting thing. Unfortunately, she couldn't contradict him with any real conviction, because she didn't remember the specifics, just the lurid generalities.

"I never would have figured you for such a wild little thing," he said, his voice still softened and husky. "You damn near wore me out."

"Stop it," she said, raising a hand. "Stop it right there. I admit that I don't remember exactly what happened in here, but that doesn't give you the right to torture me with insinuations and innuendo."

"Innuendo, hell, I can tell you exactly what we did."

"No!" She threw up a hand. "Whatever it was, it's over and done with. We can't change it now, much as I might want to."

She turned away from him, wishing she could wave a wand and vanish into thin air. It was such a comforting idea, she pulled the bedspread over her head and sank down at the same time, literally disappearing underneath it. She crouched on the floor, enveloped in darkness, determined to escape his smug smile for as long as it took her to get a grip on the situation.

"What is this? Hide-and-seek?"

It was Sam's voice. Light flooded her from behind as he picked up the other end of the spread.

"Do you mind?" she said, elbowing the material around her. "I'd like to be alone in here."

He dropped the blanket and she heard the bed creak as he sat down next to her. He was quiet for several moments, as though trying to decide what to do. When he finally spoke, the wry amusement had been tempered slightly, by qualities she never would have thought him capable of—patience, concern. "Nothing like this has ever happened to you before, has it, Lace?" he said. "Do you want to talk about it?"

Bev's heart began to pound oddly. She hesitated, then lowered the spread to look at him. Deep in his blue eyes she caught a flash of his trademark cockiness. Sam Nichols would always be Sam Nichols, but something else had crept into his expression, a hint of gravity that made him even more handsome. The scar tugged at his lower lip like a signal marker, a pointing finger. For some reason, it put her in touch with her own scars, her own invisible wounds. He wasn't capable of sensitivity, was he? Of feeling concern for her? Her throat tightened, and her heart gave a quick, wrenching thud. Because if he was capable of those things, she wasn't sure she could stop herself from getting involved.

"No, I don't want to talk," she said quickly, wishing the tight sensation in her throat would go away. Feelings were stirring inside her that she didn't want to acknowledge, tender feelings that were completely inappropriate in a situation like this. She gathered the blanket around her, shaking off his attempt to help her as she rose awkwardly to her feet.

"Are you okay?" he asked.

"I'm fine." She looked up, drawn by the worried tone in his voice and the questions in his eyes. "Is something wrong? Why are you staring at me like that?"

Sam was trying to make sense of her behavior. There *was* something bothering her, something so personal she couldn't open up about it. "You said you were married once, didn't you? And divorced?"

"Yes . . . why?"

"Divorce can be rough." He drew the sheet around himself, buying some time before he went on. "I've been that route too. I just wondered if your breakup had anything to do with sex. You know, making love?"

Bev felt a sparkle of panic. "Why would you think that?"

"I don't know. . . ." He hesitated, then shrugged it off. "No reason, I guess. Maybe I'm out of line."

"Did something happen while we were making love? Did I say . . . or do something?"

He shook his head, but Bev didn't believe him. She must have revealed something. Why else had he asked? Lord, she felt like a fool. She'd had the most intimate physical experience of a woman's life, and she couldn't remember what she'd said or done. But what disturbed her even more was that he *did* know.

"Last night was a mistake, Sam," she said abruptly. "One thing led to another, and we got a little carried away. All right, that happens. We're consenting adults. But it *was* a mistake." She eyed him sharply. "And I'm sure we would both be terribly embarrassed if anyone else found out about it. Arthur, for example. It could blow the Covington case, and then my father would demand an explanation."

Sam felt a twinge of guilt. If she'd wanted to prod his conscience, she'd picked the one thing that would work. She was Harve Brewster's kid, and he'd made Harve a promise. He was also feeling a little uncomfortable about the wildness of their lovemaking. There'd been something too urgent about the way she'd wanted him to "do it all" to her, as though she had something to prove.

"Maybe we could just forget this whole thing, huh, Sam?" she suggested, her voice softened, taking on a wheedling tone. "After all, I was under the influence of a chemical substance, and therefore . . . not myself."

She peered at him from over the top of the blanket, her big gray eyes trying to convince him that she was a wronged woman, an innocent victim of circumstances, that it had all been the booze.

He leaned back on his elbows, aware of a tight sensation in his chest. She was asking him to play along, to pretend that what they'd done had meant nothing. And for some reason he couldn't fathom at the moment. That hurt. "Let me get this straight. You're saying you wouldn't have done it if you hadn't been drunk?"

She nodded.

"And that you didn't enjoy it?"

She began to nod again.

"Like hell," he said quietly. "You had a whale of a time, lady. I was there, remember? And as long as we're talking about it, let's set the record straight. You were no victim of circumstances either. You were exactly where you wanted to be. You've been hot to get physical since the day we met in the bar."

"Hot to get physical?"

He nodded at her slowly. "Don't tell me you haven't been curious about what I'd be like in the sack. I've seen that wistful look in your eyes, that sexy question mark. You were dying to know what kind of thrills a rowdy like Sam Nichols had in store."

"I was *not* hot to get physical!"

Sam rolled his eyes. He would never understand women. They couldn't handle the simple biological truth. People got turned on. They had sex. It was all hormones and biochemistry. Why did women have to romanticize everything and make it meaningful? They couldn't even admit to wanting what they wanted. "Have it your way," he said finally.

A faintly metallic taste was in his mouth as he turned away from B.J. Brewster's self-proclaimed innocence. She might be Harve's daughter, but from where he sat, she wasn't all that different from the other lace collars he'd known. She'd gotten drunk, played out one of her secret fantasies, and now she wanted to forget the whole damn thing. She probably wanted to forget he existed. Well, so be it. They were right back where they started—partners on one of the most asinine cases he'd ever been involved in.

"You agree, then?" she said, surprise in her voice. "We can put this behind us, forget it happened?"

"You already have, right?" He raked a hand through his hair. "Yeah, sure."

As she turned away and began riffling through her suitcase for clothes, Sam grabbed a pair of jeans out of his duffel bag and pulled them on. As he buttoned the fly, he couldn't help remembering their steamy encounter in the shower, and his thoughts took a cynical twist. Why did women always seem to want what they couldn't have? The street-savvy women he had something in common with rarely looked at him with that flicker of sexual longing in their eyes. It was always the nice chicks—like her—who undressed him with their eyes, who secretly fantasized about an erotic detour from the predictable path of their predictable lives. He didn't like being a diversion. He didn't like it at all.

Suddenly he felt like a drink. As he pulled on his T-shirt and began the search for his shoes, he noticed the small box Bev held in her hand. She was reading the label of what looked like a prescription drug. The first thing that popped into his head was birth control. "Is there a problem?" he asked. "Are you protected?"

She turned abruptly, her face pale. "Birth control? Why did you ask?"

He indicated the box she was holding. "We didn't stop long enough to take any precautions. If there's a problem—"

"Don't worry about it," she said, cutting him off sharply. "I'm well protected."

Bev couldn't imagine why she felt insulted by his question, but she did. If that wasn't just like a man, she thought, tossing the seasickness prescription back into her suitcase. They certainly had a way of boiling sexual intimacy down to its lowest common denominator—in this case, her reproductive cycle.

She began tidying up the cabin, picking up clothes, mostly Sam's, and stuffing them into the ship's plastic laundry bag. Her ex-husband had been obsessed because she couldn't get pregnant. Now Sam Nichols was already getting paranoid because he thought she might be. Some women would have been pleased that he'd even mentioned birth control, but it felt too much like clinical detachment to her—and it hurt.

"What the hell's wrong now?" he asked softly.

"Nothing." She bent and picked up a damp article of clothing, holding it away from her as she realized it was her plum-stained panties. "This was a ghastly mistake, that's all."

If the first week of the cruise had sailed by in a giddy whirl, the second chugged so slowly, Bev had begun to think they'd hit a sandbar. Time crawled by on all fours and the weather turned steam-bath hot. Nights in her cracker box of a cabin were nearly unbearable without air-conditioning, and Bev's insomnia was relentless. Of course, she couldn't actually have counted every tick of the clock, night and day, and noted every rising notch of the thermometer, but it seemed that way.

The situation with Sam was equally unbearable. They'd been giving each other a wide berth, in every sense of that phrase, but it would never be wide enough. Bev was constantly searching her memory trying to recall what had happened between them. She would never have any peace of mind until she knew.

Whenever she showered or dressed, she found marks on her body in the most embarrassing places—little bruises that looked suspiciously like teeth marks. Love bites? The thought left her lightheaded and slightly horrified. The nights she did sleep, fitfully, she had dreamlike flashes of such vibrancy, she woke up drenched with perspiration.

Her stomach muscles would clutch the moment she sat up, and her thighs would ache with an intensity that made her want to moan aloud. Her wild night with Sam seemed to have set a strange and feverish physical chain reaction in motion.

Even during the day she had a fiery ache inside that built to a crescendo whenever she glimpsed Sam. It was as though he'd given her body a taste of something so powerful it could never forget—and yet her mind refused to let her remember! What had they done? She wanted to ask him, to get the torment over with, but her pride wouldn't let her. Asking for that kind of information would make her much too vulnerable to him.

Sam probably wouldn't have told her if she had asked. He wasn't trying to remember, he was trying to forget. His hormones were exacting their own brand of punishment for his sexual escapades. Since they'd happened, he'd been sleeping on the cabin floor, as far away from her as he could get, but that didn't stop him from waking up mornings in a physical state that would have hobbled a bull elephant. And it didn't stop his imagination from working overtime, cooking up a return engagement with her.

He didn't want to get near her—especially after the all-innocence routine she'd pulled—and yet he was aching to be with her again, even just to touch her, if that was all he could have. He kept conjuring up ways to accidentally brush past her, to catch a whiff of her scent, to touch her hair. It was childish. He hadn't been reduced to planning "accidental" meetings since second grade, when his dream had been to hold Lucy Delasandro's hand in a movie.

Sometimes he thought his mind was going, and he knew without doubt that his health was deteriorating. His throat was dry and scratchy, his palms were sweaty. He was hyper all night, bushed all day. His nervous system was totally out of whack, and the whole damn mess had him wound up as tight as the peel on an apple.

As luck would have it, he was in exactly that state of mind when he next ran into Bev outside their torture chamber. It was late in the week, just two days before the cruise was to end, and he was climbing an inside stairway that led to the sun deck.

She was coming down. It was one of those narrow passageways the crew used, where only one could pass comfortably. Somebody had to give, but the moment Sam saw Bev, he stopped, refusing to back down. His heart was pounding like a kid's. He had her now. That thought flashed blindingly in his mind.

"I was just going down to the cabin to get some sun block," she said, her voice quick and raspy. The sound of it sent an odd flare of longing through him. The sensation was quick and fierce, so strangely sweet, it paralyzed him for a moment. And then the familiar ache of tautening muscles hit his groin and radiated down his legs. What was this woman doing to him?

She was on the step just above him, which brought their eyes almost level, until he moved up and joined her. All the air in the corridor seemed to evaporate as he placed his hand against the wall above her head. She leaned back, her breath suspended as she glanced up and met his eyes.

"We agreed we weren't going to do this," she said.

"We did, yes."

They had agreed. No more sex. He had promised not to touch her, but none of that seemed to matter as he stared down at her. A faint pulse was fluttering in her throat, and her eyes sparkled with quicksilver excitement. He wanted to touch her. He wanted to kiss her. God help him, he wanted to drag her into his arms and never let her go.

"We're in a stairw-way," she said. "Anyone could walk in on us."

"I don't care where we are." He bent his head, heard her soft, torn moan, and felt his guts turning into mush. He'd barely touched her parted lips when the paralyzing sensation hit him again, so unexpectedly that for a moment he couldn't breathe. What in the hell?

A wave of warmth washed over him, deepening the pounding of his heart, which seemed about to leap out of his chest. He felt as though he were sinking in quicksand. What was going on? He pushed back abruptly, and stared at her.

"What's wrong?" she said.

"Nothing." He was having a heart attack, that was what was wrong. She was turning him into a cardiac case. Five more minutes of this and he'd be on the floor. "What are you doing to me?" he said, searching her face.

"I'm not doing anything, Sam. I'm not even touching you. You look pale," she pressed. "What is it?"

"I don't feel . . . right." There were things going on inside him he'd never experienced before. His stomach had turned into a carnival ride. He had to get some air to breathe, some space. He had to find some solid ground to stand on.

"Sam, where are you going? Let me help—"

"No, don't help me," he said, waving her away as he backed down the stairway. "Don't even think about helping me." When he reached the door at the bottom, he glanced up dizzily at her dumbfounded expression. "You get near me again and I'm a dead man."

Ten

" 'Put it in your bra'?" Bev grumbled aloud as she fiddled with the surveillance microphone Sam had given her moments earlier. He'd jury-rigged the tiny device so that she could conceal it under her strapless dress, and then he'd made a quick exit, refusing to have anything to do with her efforts to get it attached. "Sure, like it was easy or something," she said, trying to fasten delicate wires to sheer black lace.

She was beginning to feel like a typhoid carrier, the way Sam was acting. They may have agreed to stay away from each other, but he was being ridiculous. He'd moved his things out of the cabin, saying only that he was sleeping in a storage room somewhere. She'd insisted it was unnecessary, arguing that they were both adults and could control their biological urges. He'd told her to speak for her own urges.

After another moment or two of maneuvering, Bev had the microphone attached. She checked herself out in the mirror and nodded approvingly. Arthur would be too distracted by the slinky black strapless dress she'd borrowed from Tina to notice a minute bubble in the clingy fabric of the bodice.

She glanced at her watch. "Five minutes to zero hour."

She was meeting Arthur in moments, and that night was terribly important. The ship was docked in Nassau for the last evening of the cruise, and Arthur had invited her ashore for dinner. Instead of a restaurant, he'd made arrangements for the meal to be served in the penthouse apartment of a luxury hotel so they could have privacy. He'd told her at lunch, very mysteriously, that he had something important to discuss with her, a proposal that would affect both their futures.

Sam was sure Arthur had taken the bait and was going to try to entice Bev into an investment scam. If he did, Bev was supposed to express strong interest, and then suggest that Arthur return to the States with her, where she would withdraw the necessary cash from a trust account. Lydia Covington would be waiting in her Key West villa for word of her runaway husband's return.

As she locked the cabin door behind her, she felt triumphant in having Arthur so close to where they wanted him. It still amazed her that such a sweet, sensitive man was a con artist. He certainly knew how to use his poetic nature to his advantage. If she hadn't known all about him, she would have eagerly swallowed all his flattery. Unlike some men, Arthur understood how to make a woman feel totally appreciated for her feminine qualities.

"He could give Sam Nichols a few lessons in how to treat a woman," she said, a taut sigh in her voice. She fingered the tiny device in her bodice and a pensive smile flickered on her lips. She was wearing a wire. Sam would be listening to the whole thing.

"'She walks in beauty, like the night/Of cloudless climes and starry skies . . .'"

Bev set down her champagne flute as Arthur let the words trail off. "Shelley?" she asked.

"Byron."

"Oh, yes, of course. How could I have forgotten? It's

one of his most popular poems." Arthur had been quoting poetry and sending Bev adoring smiles across the dinner table all evening. He was building to a proposal, all right, but she doubted it had anything to do with her finances. She glanced at the concealed microphone in her dress, wondering if Sam was listening.

"'And all that's best of dark and bright/Meet in her aspect and her eyes . . .'"

Bev's fingernails did a nervous tap dance against the rim of the glass as Arthur droned on. She loved romantic poetry as well as the next person, but he was showing no signs of letting up. Somehow she had to get him off Byron and onto the mysterious reason he'd invited her.

"'Thus mellow'd to that tender light/Which heaven to gaudy day deni—'"

"Arthur." She smiled apologetically and softened her tone as he stopped short, open-mouthed. "Arthur, wasn't there something you wanted to talk about?"

"Talk? Oh, I—" He blushed to the roots of his silver hair, and Bev felt frustrated. She'd embarrassed him again. Even an offhand smile could embarrass Arthur, and then he'd stumble and bumble forever, helpless to recover his composure.

"It's all right," she said quickly. "We don't have to talk if you'd rather not. Here, have some more champagne." She sprang up and walked around the table, plucking the magnum from its bucket and splashing some bubbly into Arthur's glass.

"No! I do, I mean I want to t-talk." Arthur nearly tipped his chair over as he rose and picked up his champagne glass. "Toast?" he said.

"Toast? Oh . . . toast. Sure." Bev hurried to get her glass, filling it as she walked back to him. "That's a lovely idea. Let's have a toast."

Their glasses hit with a clink loud enough to crack the crystal. "Oops," Arthur said, his eyes lighting up with startled laughter. "Don't know my own strength."

Bev was laughing too as she tipped the brimming glass to her lips. Champagne bubbled up and spilled over, running down her neck in rivulets that made a beeline for her cleavage.

"Oh, I'm sorry!" Arthur gasped.

"It was me," Bev assured him. "I'm jinxed when it comes to alcohol." She took the napkin he thrust at her, still laughing softly as she daubed at herself.

"Bev . . . ?"

"Yes?" Still daubing, she looked up and saw the horrified expression on Arthur's face.

"What is that?" He was pointing at her chest.

A black spidery thing had attached itself to Bev's napkin. She let out a shriek and flipped the napkin onto the table.

"I've got it!" Arthur grabbed his coffee cup and hero-ically stomped the grotesque insect.

"Arthur!" Bev had never seen him so dynamic and forceful. She was about to congratulate him, when a high-pitched tone pierced her ears. "What's that noise?" she said, looking around. Static crackled and popped, drawing her back to the squashed bug on the table. She gaped at it, giving out another soft shriek as she realized what it was. Her surveillance microphone!

Somehow the device must have gotten hooked on the napkin and she'd pulled it out of her bra! Worse, it was shorting out!

Arthur was staring at the device suspiciously. "Bev? What is this thing?" He poked at it with his dinner fork, and finally he scooped it up in his palm for a closer look. "It's a microphone, isn't it?" he said, looking up at her. "A bug?" His expression was that of a confused, wounded child.

Bev sighed. "It *was* a microphone."

"You were recording our conversation?"

"Oh, Arthur . . . I can explain."

Fifteen minutes later, seated on the penthouse's liv-ing room couch with Arthur, Bev had told him pretty much the whole story, including the fact that she was a private detective. She was sure she was violating every precious tenet of Sam's standard operating procedure, but there was no way to get out of it. If Arthur decided to threaten her, she could hold him at bay until Sam came. And she hoped he would soon. He'd probably guessed something was wrong as soon as her microphone went dead, and even if he had avoided her lately, he would come to her rescue. Wouldn't he?

"A private detective, really?" Arthur said amazed. "You're very good."

"Do you think so?" If she kept him talking, she might be able to make him confess. And timid soul that he was, she might even be able to convince him to return to the United States.

"Oh, yes," Arthur said, absolutely sincere. "I would never have guessed you for a flatfoot. And I can usually tell." He scratched his head, and smiled at her, perplexed. "The problem now is what to do with you. I don't think I've ever been in this predicament before."

"Arthur," Bev said with a motherly pat to his hand. "That's sweet, but you shouldn't be worrying about me right now. You need to concentrate on resolving the situation with Lydia. I want you to think seriously about meeting with her, Arthur. She's promised not to prosecute if you return the money."

"Oh, I couldn't go back."

"Arthur, now, listen to me. If you don't go back, she's going to notify the police, and you know how they are. They'll drag in the F.B.I. There'll be machine guns and S.W.A.T. teams—"

"No, you don't understand, Bev," he said. "I *can't* go back. I don't have the money. I really did invest it. I wasn't trying to hurt Lydia, I love Lydia. I love all rich women. I was only trying to make her richer." He raised his hands helplessly.

"Oh . . . dear." Bev rose from the couch and walked to the penthouse windows, wondering where Sam was. "I'm sorry," she said, staring out at the lights of Nassau, "but it looks like you're going to have to go back and face this thing, Arthur. I don't see any other way. Life isn't a cruise ship cocktail lounge. You can't run a tab forever."

She turned back, determined to persuade him.

"Arthur?"

He was holding a gun on her, a very large gun!

He looked like a repentant puppy dog, all sad eyes and imploring shrugs. "I'm sorry too, Bev. I feel just terrible about this, but I'm going to have to tie you up."

In a room below the penthouse, Sam was checking out the deafening static on his receiver. He'd just upgraded his equipment, it was state of the art technology, and he was seriously ticked off that it wasn't working.

"Hell with it," he muttered finally. He would have to do his eavesdropping first-hand.

He ran up the stairs and walked quietly down the hallway to the penthouse door. He picked the lock and crept into the living room just in time to hear Bev tell Arthur what a wonderful guy he was and begging him not to waste himself. Arthur humbly protested, insisting that Bev was the one who was wonderful. Sam rolled his eyes. They had a real mutual admiration society going. Bev was coming off like a self-esteem counselor. It was a novel approach to dealing with a four-flushing chiseler.

"I like you, Bev," Arthur said, his voice raspy with emotion. "Very much. I wish it didn't have to be this way. I wish we'd met under other circumstances. I wish—"

"Oh, Arthur—"

The room went silent, and Sam's senses went on alert. What was going on in there? He inched forward, heard a funny, breathy sound, like a sigh, and his imagination caught fire. What was that poetry-puking little bastard doing? Kissing her?

Sam swung into the room, his fists clenched. He hesitated, confused at the sight of Bev standing across the room by the couch. She was alone. Where was Arthur?

"Bad timing, Sam," Bev said, indicating that someone was behind him. Sam whirled and came face-to-face with the barrel of a 9mm Beretta. He raised his hands slowly. Suckered by Arthur Blankenship? He really was losing it.

"Boy, what a mess, huh?" Arthur shrugged apologetically. "Now I'm going to have to tie you up too."

Sam's upper lip curled, a predatory snarl. "Never gonna happen."

"Sam," Bev pointed out hastily, "Arthur does have a gun."

Arthur stepped back, aiming the barrel at a very vulnerable part of Sam's body. "Stay where you are," he warned, squinting at Sam's surly features. "Say . . . aren't you the waiter?"

"Actually, he's—" Bev started.

"I'm her partner," Sam cut in. "And if you try any more of that touchy-feely stuff with her, you're a dead con man."

Arthur blanched. "Bev," he said, "do as I tell you. Quickly. Take the cord from the drapes and use it to tie Sam's hands and feet."

Sam moved imperceptibly, looking for an opening. Arthur frantically released the gun's safety, shrieking as a crack of light and sound exploded. A bullet hit the wall unit behind Sam.

"My God, it went off!" Arthur breathed.

"I hate it when that happens," Sam growled, ducking as Arthur looked up. "Hey! Watch where you're pointing that thing!"

Fifteen minutes later Sam Nichols was lying on the penthouse floor, bound and trussed like a rodeo steer. Bev, having done most of the binding and trussing, had returned to the sofa. Her ears were still burning from Sam's profane mutterings. "Nice work, Bev," Arthur said, checking Sam's knots. "I'm afraid it's your turn now. I'd like you to lie down, facing Sam, your hands behind your back."

A gasp caught in Bev's throat. "Arthur, please! You're not going to tie me to him?" In her panic she recklessly considered rushing Arthur and trying to disarm him.

Bev was praying for a catastrophic act of nature by the time Arthur got done lashing her to Sam Nichols. Sam was grimly silent through the whole thing. And Arthur, sensitive to Bev's distress, apologized repeatedly for any inconvenience he was causing her.

"I'm going to put out the Do Not Disturb sign," Arthur told them moments later as he was preparing to leave. "But don't worry. Someone will come up to investigate when you don't check out tomorrow at noon." He smiled hopefully, indicating the suite. "It's a beautiful suite, isn't it? I guess if you have to be tied up somewhere, it might as well be the penthouse."

With one last contrite farewell, Arthur left.

"If we ever get out of this place," Sam grated, twisting against his bonds, "remind me to change my profession. Con men know how to live. Women, money—must be nice."

Beth sighed impatiently. "First, you'll have to learn how to treat a woman, Sam Nichols. Arthur's a successful con man because he knows a woman wants to feel needed, and he—"

Sam jettisoned a four-letter word that made Bev wince.

A tense silence followed. Bev weighed the odds of trying to defuse the situation and decided it was too risky. Being tied to Sam was like being tied to live explosives. There was no escape if she accidentally set him off again.

Arthur had arranged them so that her face nuzzled into the curve of Sam's neck. There was something incredibly awkward—and intimate—about the position, but at least she didn't have to look at him. Everywhere else they were sealed together like a Ziploc bag.

Bev felt a flush of awareness warm her throat. In the crush of their bodies, she could discern the scars on his chest, the buttons of his fly, and especially his hip-bones, one of which happened to be nestled intimately in the curve of her pelvis.

There'd been nothing stimulating about being tied to him at first. *Au contraire*. But now that she was becoming aware of his various parts, and of where those parts were touching her parts—

She tried to cancel out the thought, but it was too late. Her senses had been awakened. She was unavoidably aware of him now. Her body had been alerted, and it was buzzing from head to toe with information her mind couldn't turn off.

"Any ideas on how to get free?" she asked, speaking into Sam's shirt collar.

"I've been thinking about nothing else," he said tightly. "If we can get ourselves turned around, we can use our hands to untie each other."

"Why don't we just yell?" Bev suggested. "Someone will hear us eventually."

"Not a chance. We're on the top floor of the hotel, and this joint is soundproof. We've got to get turned around. It's the only way."

The ropes were too tight for them both to turn at once, so Bev went first. Without the use of her hands, all she could do was wriggle and squirm. In her worst nightmare she couldn't have imagined a more embarrassing situation. Sam was pretending not to notice her gyrations, but the way he was gritting his teeth told her he hated every frustrating second of it. He was acting as though he were in mortal pain.

If Sam wasn't in mortal pain, he was close to it. He had made himself a solemn promise that he would never lay a hand on Bev Brewster again, and here he was, lashed to her squirming body. He'd been stomped and shot and spurned in his life, but this fiasco was the Super Bowl of torture. It made him wonder whether he'd laughed in the face of fate one too many times.

"Take it easy," he said as her knee dug the inside of his thigh. She was perilously close to his groin, and the way she was thrashing, she was going to maim him for life. Not only that, her chin felt as though it had made a permanent indentation in his chest, her hair was in his face. And her breasts were all over him!

He probably could have held out indefinitely if it hadn't been for her breasts. Her strapless dress was inching down with each move she made. Even with his eyes shut, he could feel the weight and warmth of her spilling against him. She was perspiring lightly, and the moisture collecting in the groove of her collarbones and the cleft of her breasts gave off a scent that was distinctly female. It aroused every normal male instinct he had.

Should he mention that she was undressing herself? His conscience told him to stop her—for both their sakes—but the darker side of his personality told him to shut up.

Her next contortion revealed more creamy flesh and a glimpse of rosy areola. Sam's heart started to pound. Heart attack time. "Hold it," he said abruptly. "There's got to be an easier way to do this. You hold still, and I'll turn."

"I'm not stopping now." Bev had a system going, an ingenious sequence of pelvic thrusts, swim kicks, and shoulder rotations. "This is working, Sam. I'm about a quarter of the way."

"Yeah, but your dress isn't making the trip with you."

She glanced down and saw the problem. One more shoulder rotation and she was topless! It was a disconcerting prospect, but she'd gone too far to give up. After more twisting and arching her back, she finally managed to bring up most of the clingy material with her.

"Congratulations," Sam said dryly.

She met his dazzling blue eyes and smiled. "Right, like you really wanted me to solve the problem."

By the time Bev was completely turned around, she had an even larger problem. Her bound hands were planted firmly in an unusually hard area of his body, and though she hoped it was his muscled stomach, she had a sinking suspicion it wasn't. Her own stomach churned as she touched and patted gingerly, trying to confirm what she was actually feeling.

Sam made a strange sound as she discerned something long and solid through the material of his jeans. A light flashed on in her mind, illuminating a dark corner of her memory. She was in a shower, drenched and slightly drunk, unbuttoning a man's jeans, touching him, arousing him, bending to kiss—no!

"Don't move a muscle," Sam said, his neck tendons bulging like cables. "Don't even breathe. I think I've exceeded my minimum daily requirement of foreplay."

"I'm sorry," Bev said faintly. "I wasn't trying to turn you on, it's just this—"

"Of course you weren't trying to turn me on. You're never trying, and yet for some reason my pants haven't fit right since the day I met you. How do you explain that? If you're not trying, what in the hell are you doing, woman?"

"I had no idea Arthur was going to tie us up together. Surely you're not blaming me for that."

Given his state of mind and body, Sam was ready to blame her for everything. His blood was pounding in his veins, and his guts were in knots, which didn't surprise him. He'd been in knots for days, one damn way or another. He was torn between a desire to drag her into his arms and kiss the sap out of her and to storm out of her life forever. Right. With his hands and feet tied behind his back?

"I've had it," he said, checking out the room. "I'm going to get us out of this mess. There's a telephone on that table. If we can knock it to the floor, we can get the switchboard operator."

"Okay, but how do we get there?"

"Roll."

Roll they did. Whatever notion Bev had of protecting her dignity was lost long ago—when her dress took a detour and her hands got waylaid on his crotch. Just keep moving, she told herself.

Sam knew he was in trouble when he wanted to stop moving. The sensation of her body sliding over his, and then under his, and then over his again, was enough to arouse the libido of a hibernating grizzly. His heart was a jackhammer and his groin was one huge muscle spasm. He just knew he was going to suffer a heart attack and die before they got to the phone, but he wasn't sure he gave a damn. He would check out a happy man.

In the course of their dizzy journey, his animal passions had taken over. His imagination had them making wild love as they rolled across the room. He was holding her, moving deeply inside her, reveling in the feel of her legs wrapped around his waist and the sweet bounce of her butt as she swung on top of him.

By the time they got to the phone Sam was so crazed with lustful thoughts, he'd forgotten all about his plan. He wrenched at their bonds, desperate to haul her into his arms. Desperate to get at her!

Bev didn't have the strength to help him. Between their feverish trip across the room and his powerful efforts to free them, she was dizzy with excitement. Her heart was out of control, and her legs were already melting, aching, throbbing for that moment when he would open them. But a part of her was fighting the inevitable, resisting the erotic chaos that overwhelmed her when she was with him.

If Sam sensed her conflict, he was too agonizingly aroused to respond to it. Somehow, their movements had loosened the ropes, and the knots around his wrists gave way as he tugged against them, releasing one of his hands. "I'm free, Lace," he said huskily, turning her around to face him.

She refused to look at him, and as he stared at her in confusion, he realized her dress was down around her waist. She was lying on her side, and seeing the graceful slope of her breasts sent a flash of awareness through him. She was half naked and irresistible. She was beautiful and vulnerable.

He pushed back, straining against the bonds. "What is it?" he asked. "What's wrong?"

She heaved a sigh and forced herself to look at him. "You and me, Sam. It's us. We're like animals in heat the way we go at each other. I didn't want it to happen that way again. It's not right."

"We're not going at each other."

"I know . . . but we will be in a minute." Her eyes breathed fire as she gazed at him. "I want you, Sam," she said. "I wish I didn't, but I do."

He touched her then. He caressed her cheek with his free hand, racked by a tenderness he didn't understand. "Oh, man," he said softly, "why are you so damn beautiful? Why are your breasts naked? And why am I so crazy about you, Lace? Why do I need you?"

His voice trailed off in a husky groan, but Bev had heard the word *need,* and it sent a burst of longing through her. The sudden deep ache in her loins was almost unbearable. "Get us out of these ropes, Sam."

A crazy thought flashed into her head as he fought with their bonds. They were going to miss their boat. She ought to tell him. If the cruise ship left without them, Arthur would get away. But she didn't breathe a word of it as he flung away the last of the cording and dragged her into his arms. The sound that came out of him was so filled with passion and need, so rich with male relief, it brought tears to her eyes. She wasn't the only one hurting.

In his haste he'd freed only one of her hands, but it was all she needed. She clutched at the straining muscles of his back, locking herself to him with a muted cry that was softly jubilant.

He kissed her deeply, his mouth hungry on hers. His tongue stroked over her teeth and the inner lining of her lips, then dipped inside, sliding hotly against her tongue. She could feel him pulling deeply on her, drinking in her sweetness as though he wanted to draw her into him and consume her. His rough passion might have frightened her if it hadn't been exactly what she needed.

His raw masculinity made her want to be swept up by the forces that drove him. Even the reckless way he urged her legs apart made her yearn for the hard, quick thrust of his body. She wanted to be shattered by passion!

He broke their kiss with a sound of rampant dissatisfaction, lifted her bodily, and peeled off her clingy dress with one continuous stroke. Her underwear went next, and then he tore at the buttons on his fly in frustration, not bothering to take the jeans off.

Poised between her thighs, he caught hold of her face, framing it with a fierce, tender grip. "Wrap your legs around me, Lace. Do it now."

She clung to him with her thighs, excitement streaming up her legs. The sensations were so vibrant, they made her weak with anticipation. "Hold me," she said, gasping as he entered her. "Dance with me." He drove deeply and the power of his body sent shock waves of pleasure through her.

This couldn't be wrong, she thought. Nothing had ever felt so right. He was rough and hungry and dominant by nature. He was even crude, but no one had ever made her feel so potent, so female. She went a little wild when she was with him, a woman out of control, but it was right. It was perfect.

As their lovemaking intensified, Bev's world became pure sensation. Colors flashed kaleidoscopically behind her closed lids and the harsh rhythm of his breathing filled her head with silver sounds. Melting pleasure radiated from that place where his body sank irresistibly into hers. Currents rippled and surged, exploding like tiny starbursts.

She was cresting, a wave about to break, when, inexplicably, he slowed and caught her up in his arms. The sudden sweetness of his need took her over the edge, and her inner world of sensation dissolved in chaos. She was tumbling over a waterfall, buffeted by raging currents, dragged under by ecstasy. The journey swept her along, taking everything she had.

It wasn't until he was holding her afterward that Sam realized he hadn't released one of her hands. He looked at her, his expression holding concern, even tenderness. "I didn't hurt you, did I? Are you all right?"

"No and yes," she said, a smile sparkling. "I'm not just okay, I'm hopelessly content. All I want to do now is lie in your arms. I want to sleep with you, Sam."

He scooped her up from the floor and rose to his feet without even a grimace of pain. "There's a bedroom at the end of the hallway."

The room he spoke of so casually was a huge chamber of black marble and faux leopardskin prints. The canopied bed was enveloped in sheer black mosquito netting, and the bed sheets were made of the softest, densest silk.

The world seemed a perfect place as she snuggled into the curve of Sam's arm moments later. Even the fact that they'd let Arthur go didn't matter. How could the case of the romantic con man and his still-infatuated victim compare to the bliss she was feeling for the first time in her life?

Eleven

Feeling as though she were swimming in jasmine-scented silk, Bev stretched languorously from head to toe. She was drifting toward consciousness, but she didn't want to wake up yet. The misty veil of sleep seemed a protection from something she didn't want to acknowledge.

Rolling to her side, she nestled into the pillowcase, opened one eye lazily . . . and saw the very thing she was trying to avoid. Sam Nichols was sound asleep next to her, his head partially covered by a pillow in a leopardskin case.

Bev pressed her face into her own pillow. It wasn't a dream. It had all happened. Arthur had tied them up and made his escape the previous night. She and Sam had made love, once on the floor, twice more in this enormous bed. Afterward, they'd fallen asleep exhausted.

Her groan was muffled by her pillow. They'd fallen asleep instead of going after Arthur. Instead of catching the next plane to Fort Lauderdale to intercept the cruise ship's arrival. Her misjudgment sent her into a tailspin of concern about letting down her father and Lydia Covington. But strangely enough, as much as that prospect disturbed her, it wasn't what was bothering her most.

Earlier that morning, near dawn, she'd awakened with a plan in her head. Why couldn't they hire a private plane and beat the cruise ship to Fort Lauderdale? she'd told Sam. She knew it was a long shot even before he vetoed the idea and drowsily pulled her into his arms. He'd been such an adorable sleepyhead, all warm and cuddly and naked, she hadn't been able to resist him.

Their lovemaking had been wonderful. Too wonderful, that was the problem. He'd been gentle, and so unexpectedly sensitive to her needs that she was moved nearly to tears. She had opened to him emotionally, surrendering her defenses in what must have been a desperate need for affirmation. When he told her how beautiful she was, she had cried. Worse, she had said things, sweet, reckless things that afterward she wished she could take back.

Now she tried to remember the words she'd used, the context, and all she knew for sure was that she had exposed too much. She had spoken from her heart, impetuously, foolishly. She'd said something about not wanting to be with any other man but him, about needing him in her life. She'd even revealed her fear that she might be falling in love with him.

Careful not to wake him, she sat up, holding the sheet to her breasts. She couldn't shake the feeling that she'd made a total fool of herself, that Sam must think she was desperate. And she had no idea how to repair the damage.

Moments later, casting about for something to put on, she found a courtesy terry robe in the hotel bathroom. Though it was far too big, she wrapped herself in it and walked to the bedroom's terrace door. The view was magnificent. The hotel overlooked a turquoise cove where transparent waters shimmered gently, but Bev was barely conscious of it.

The questions taking shape in her mind had transfixed her. Was she afraid of falling in love with Sam? Or afraid because she *was* in love with him? Had it already gone too far?

A soft musical sound interrupted Bev's turmoil. She turned, confused, and saw a gleaming marble box on the night table next to the bed. As the chimes continued, she realized it was a telephone. She couldn't imagine who knew where they were. Lydia? Her father?

She wasn't eager to talk to either of them. How could she ever explain what had happened? As she forced herself to replay the steps of her investigation, trying to formulate some reasonable defense, reality crashed down on her. There was no way to explain it. Arthur was gone. They'd blown it. *She'd* blown it, because that was how her father and Lydia would see it. She represented Brewster's, not Sam.

She opened the marble lid and stared at the sleek black receiver a moment before picking it up. "Yes?"

"B-Bev?"

The stumbling voice sent a shot of adrenaline through her. *"Arthur?"*

"I—I hoped you'd still be there, Bev. I'm sorry—"

"No, Arthur, it's all right! Where are you?"

"In Key West . . . with Lydia."

"What? You went back? That's wonderful!" Bev thought she could hear someone sobbing softly in the background. "Who's crying, Arthur? Is that Lydia? Is she all right?"

"She's overcome, Bev, with happiness. We've been talking for hours, and we've decided to try it again. I promised I'd see a psychiatrist, and of course, I'll join Con Artists Anonymous, if there is such a thing."

Bev could hardly contain herself. As relieved as she was that she and Sam hadn't blown the case, it was far more important to her that Arthur had turned out to be an honorable man! She felt as though her professional judgment had been vindicated. "What about the money, Arthur? How did you handle that?"

"I'm going to get a job as soon as I'm rehabilitated. Lydia has some contacts in the investment counseling industry back in Beverly Hills, but I think I'll hang out my own shingle."

"Attaboy! I can't wait to tell Sam!"

"Oh, S-Sam. How is Sam? He didn't look very happy last night."

Bev glanced over at the man she'd just spent the most torrid night of her life with. He was stretched out on the bed like a sleek, muscular panther, sleeping contentedly in the morning sun. "I'd say he looks happy this morning, Arthur. Very happy."

"You two worked out your differences?"

Soft laughter filled the line. "We did, yes. In a big way. You may have done us a favor, Arthur."

Bev was bursting with relief and excitement by the time she hung up the phone. "Sam!" she cried, climbing onto the bed to shake him awake. "That was Arthur! Everything's all right."

"Get off me, woman," he mumbled, "or you're a wet spot on the floor."

Undaunted, Bev began to tickle him. "Come on, Mr. Tough Guy. Wake up! Everything's—oops!"

Bev had never been athletic, but she flipped onto her back like a pancake as Sam reared up. "What are you doing?" he asked, still half asleep. He raked a mop of tousled dark hair from his eyes, looking very naked and very sexy as he stared down at Bev's helpless attempts to smother her own laughter.

"Nobody violates my armpits, babe," he warned.

"I guess Mr. Tough Guy is ticklish."

A raffish grin surfaced and his eyes glinted with dangerous lights. "She dares to mock Mr. Tough Guy? Let's see if the lady flatfoot can take what she dishes out."

Bev screamed "uncle!" before Sam had even touched her, but he straddled her anyway, yanking loose the tie on her bathrobe. He tickled her until she couldn't breathe. And then he took advantage of her while she was still writhing helplessly. He kissed her mouth, her throat, her breasts, and on down her vibrating body until he reached her toes. But it wasn't until he returned to her weak spot—her inner thighs—that she begged him to stop. She couldn't let him make love to her, not with so many things unresolved in her mind.

He gazed down at her, his pale blue eyes indecipherable. What was behind those eyes? Did he care about her at all? Was he capable of caring? "Sam, about those things I said while we were—"

He shushed her with a touch of his fingers to her mouth. "You don't have to explain anything to me, Lace," he said quietly. "Sometimes we say things. It's okay."

He swung off her and helped her up, then settled himself against the headboard, pulling the sheet up to cover his hips. "So, what's the deal with Arthur? You said everything was all right."

"Yes, it is." Bev closed the bathrobe, her insecurities burgeoning. Why had he changed the subject so quickly? Why had he covered himself? "Arthur went back to Lydia. How about that for a surprise? He'll start therapy, and he's getting a job."

He stared at her as though he didn't believe her. "Lydia is taking Arthur back?"

"Yes. Don't you think she should?"

He snorted laughter. "Not unless she's crazy. Does she think he's actually going to change?"

Suddenly Bev felt very defensive. "Of course she does. And he will. He's motivated."

"Right, motivated by her stock portfolio."

"Sam, he told me himself that he loved her."

"Oh, babe, you heard him. He said he loved *all* rich women. What he loves is taking them to the cleaners."

"God, but you're cynical," she said softly. His flippant remarks pierced her like a knife through the heart, but it wasn't the words that stabbed her, she realized. It was his attitude. The cynicism felt like a personal affront, as though he were ridiculing her and the things she believed in. She turned away, not wanting him to see the sparkle of pain in her eyes.

"B.J.," Sam said gently, "people don't change because it's the right thing to do, or because someone else wants them to. They change when it's in their own self-interest."

She shook her head. "You're wrong. He'll change for Lydia. Arthur *will* change."

Sam shook his head. "Why the hell do women always think that?" He knew better than to pursue the argument. She needed to believe that the Arthur Blankenships of the world could be salvaged. It was a romantic illusion she cherished. She needed to believe that any man could change through the love of a good woman, no matter how low he'd sunk—including Sam Nichols.

I don't want to be with anyone else but you, Sam.

His gut knotted as those trembling words played back in his head. She'd said it as though she couldn't believe it herself. And then her voice had caught and she'd poured out more sweet, damning secrets. He'd been too blown away to respond. His throat had turned into a fist, nearly strangling him. Why me? he'd asked himself. Why would she want to go and pick a bastard like me?

He glanced over at her pensive profile and felt a sudden need to touch her. There had to be some way to ease the turmoil between them. Maybe he could make a stupid joke, or kid her about her lousy standard operating procedure. The impulse to touch her moved through him like jagged glass.

"Hey, look, maybe I am cynical, okay? It's a hazard of the trade. Most detectives don't trust their own mother."

Bev turned, surprised. That had sounded like the beginning of an apology. Hope glimmered, a dangerous emotion when dealing with a man like him. "I guess I have something to look forward to," she said. "Getting cynical, that is."

"It'll never happen. You're one of the lucky ones, born with a natural immunity."

"And you're the last cynical man?"

He laughed, an irresistibly husky sound. "I guess that makes us quite a pair."

"Are we a pair?" Bev asked. The moment she'd said it, she wanted to cut her tongue out. He looked startled, then apologetic and wary. She felt her heart twisting. What more did she need to convince her that he didn't want a relationship? His body language was screaming it. She told herself to change the subject, blow her nose, anything. But something compelled her to go on.

"How do you feel about us, Sam?"

"I think we're great together."

"You do?"

"Yeah, I do."

"Then . . . you'll want us to continue seeing each other when we get back?"

His blue gaze was noncommittal. "Do you?"

Bev hesitated for just a split second before she answered. "Yes . . . of course."

"So what are we talking about here? Dating? A meaningful relationship?" He leaned forward, draping an arm over his knee. "That would be interesting. On whose terms?"

"Terms?"

"I'm no prize, babe. Maybe you ought to think about what you'd be getting into with a no-account like me. I drink, I gamble, I drive like a trucker. When the mood strikes me, I take off for parts unknown without asking anyone's permission." He took a deep breath and shook his head as though he didn't like the sound of it any better than she did. "Sorry, Lace, but that's how it is. No one holds me accountable for the way I live but me."

Bev felt as though she'd run up several flights of stairs. Her heart was thumping, her breathing shallow. It was his recklessness that had attracted her—and now he was giving her a crash course on living with a reckless man. If he was trying to scare her off, he was doing a good job, she realized. A relationship with Sam Nichols on his terms was a sobering prospect. He was cynical by his own admission, but she could live with that. It was the rest—his moods, his stubbornness. He refused to answer to anyone. He isolated himself emotionally. He was a maverick down to the toothpicks he carried in the pocket of his leather jacket.

She hated the thought that flashed into her head next, but it wouldn't be dismissed. What would her neighbors think of a roughneck like Sam? She lived in a quiet, tree-lined suburb where toddlers rode tricycles and their dads mowed the lawn on weekends. She had always planned on having that kind of life. She still wanted it.

Sam sat quietly, watching her, saying nothing. He could see it in her eyes, the rising doubts. Their lifestyles didn't mesh, and she was trying to figure out what that meant, and how to fix it. Whatever solution she came up with might sound reasonable at first, but the price tag would be his freedom. She wasn't the type to let down her hair and just hang loose with a guy—sex for sex's sake, fun while it lasted. She'd have to marry him, reform him, turn him into a Stepford husband. That was the legacy of the "nice" gene she carried. He knew. He'd been through it before.

"Beverly Jean," he said quietly, regret burning through the huskiness. "I'm not redeemable, if that's what you're thinking. I like my beer cold, my women hot, and my cards lucky."

"*Women*? Plural?"

The hurt and disbelief that flared in her eyes was like a slap across his face. *Just tell me to go to hell, babe. Don't let yourself in for this. You don't deserve it.* His throat was tight and dry as he added, "Women, plural. That wouldn't be a problem, would it?"

Add cold-blooded womanizer to the list of his flaws, Bev thought, turning away from him. Heat seared her chest as she breathed in, the air burning a path through her lungs. He was wrong when he said she was immune to cynicism. She felt plenty bitter and cynical right now. "I had a hunch you gambled," she said, flinging his indifference right back at him. "Are you any good? Lucky at cards? Unlucky at love?"

He didn't answer her, and when she turned around, he was standing at the terrace doors, staring out. He had on his jeans and his arms were folded against his bare chest. It was an unguarded pose, no male ego at stake, no swagger. Just a solitary man with the morning sunlight playing over his face and shoulders. A proud man, and probably a good man if he would ever give himself a chance. Bev felt the sting of tears as she allowed an unwelcome thought into her awareness. She couldn't share him with other women. It would destroy her, but she wanted him desperately at that moment, even with all his flaws. He was the most desirable man she'd ever known.

"Maybe we ought to be thinking about getting back home?" he said, turning to her. He looked sad somehow, and weary.

Back home, Bev thought. Where she could feed her goldfish. Where she would never have to see Sam Nichols again.

Bev glanced at her watch, saw that it was nearly noon, and put aside the forms she'd been filling out. Harve would be in soon, minding everyone else's business and full of bluster. He'd recovered enough to return to the agency on a part-time basis, but he was spoiling for the real thing, some down-and-dirty private-eye action. He'd also been after Bev to take on a new case since she'd returned from Nassau three weeks earlier, but she'd stood her ground. She would help with the paperwork, but nothing more. She'd had enough down-and-dirty private-eye action to last her until social-security age, thank you.

Bev shut her eyes and massaged the bridge of her nose. She'd been out of sorts lately, to put it mildly. The previous week she'd had a touch of the twenty-four-hour flu that was going around. That day she could feel a headache coming on. Maybe she'd go home when Harve arrived.

The buzzing of her intercom gave her a start.

"Visitors, B.J.," Cory announced, clicking off before Bev could ask who it was.

She was adjusting her sagging shoulder pads when her office door swung open. Bev rose, astonished at the beaming couple who entered. "Arthur? Lydia? How wonderful to see you! How are you?"

"Happy," Lydia said, holding out her arms, weepy eyed. "Deliriously happy. And we owe it all to you, Bev."

Bev rushed around her desk to hug Lydia, and Arthur stood back, smiling sheepishly, shy as ever. Bev hugged him too, once she'd recovered from Lydia's exuberant embrace, and before the three of them were through with their reunion, they were all laughing and blinking away tears.

"Tell me everything!" Bev said, bringing them with her to sit on the couch. "I want to know all about your wedded bliss."

Lydia was delighted to comply. She described how she and Arthur had renewed their wedding vows in a rose garden in Key West, and their recent return to Beverly Hills. "The dogs rushed Arthur and knocked him over when we got out of the car. I've never seen them so excited. They completely ignored me!"

Bev laughed, aware that the couple's visit was just what she needed to perk her up. She'd been in a state of mourning since that disastrous day in Nassau.

"Is everything all right, dear?" Lydia patted Bev's hand as though she'd been reading her mind. "You look a little peaked."

"How's S-Sam?" Arthur broke in, his first words since he'd entered the office.

Bev toyed with the idea of telling him that Sam was fine and leaving it at that. But both he and Lydia were staring at her so intently, she found herself wanting to tell them the truth. "I don't know. I haven't seen Sam since the cruise."

Arthur went noticeably pale. "Is there a problem? Oh, dear, I hope it wasn't because of me."

Bev had never discussed what happened in Nassau with anyone, not even Harve, and she was reluctant to do so now. There was so much heartache dammed up inside her—anger, confusion, and especially hurt. She felt like the little Dutch boy in the fable who didn't dare take his finger out of the dike. Talking about Sam Nichols meant risking a flash flood, but she'd reached a point where she needed to talk to someone. And she couldn't leave Arthur thinking he was responsible.

"Sam is a man with some very deep scars," she said, choosing her words carefully. "He's afraid to let anyone close." She was referring to emotional wounds, but her mind flashed a graphic reminder of his mutilated upper body and the scar that forked from his mouth. Her throat constricted as she thought of how much pain Sam had suffered.

She glanced up to see Arthur and Lydia clasp hands. It was an instinctive reaction to her news, Bev realized. They were reaffirming their bond, reassuring each other of their devotion. At the same time that Bev was happy for them, their linked hands were a piercing reminder of her own losses.

"It's too bad Sam isn't here to see you two," she said, unable to hide her own sadness. "He pretends to have such disdain for marriage, and especially for the healing power of love. I wish he could know how happy you are."

"Sam's a fool," Arthur blurted out passionately. "What is life about if you can't share things, everything—the joy and the pain—with someone you care about?"

Bev was caught off guard by the depth of Arthur's conviction. The words ricocheted in her head, forcing her to consider them. He may have been speaking about Sam, but what he said applied to her too. She had cut herself off years earlier, right after Paul left. Her reaction had been to hole up like a hermit in her Valley home, refusing to share any of her pain. And her reaction to

Sam's rejection had been very much the same. She would have isolated herself totally if her father hadn't needed her help at the agency.

She could feel the sadness cresting inside her. All that aching emptiness, all those wasted years. "Excuse me," she said, looking away as tears threatened. It was pain from the past she was fighting. They were yesterday's tears, and they stung that much more bitterly for having been denied.

"I'm sorry—" Her voice caught as she tried to regain control. "I was afraid this might happen."

Lydia sat beside her and put an arm around her. "Is there anything we can do, Bev? Would you like us to leave?"

Bev shook her head. She wanted to fall into Lydia's arms and cry her heart out, but pride kept her rigid. "No, it's all right. Just give me a minute."

"We love you, Bev," Arthur said softly.

Bev's throat swelled with a sudden stinging heat. Their kindness was more than she could handle. She had to get out of the room or she would never get control. "Please, it's all right. I'll just go wash my face."

A wave of dizziness swept her as she stood up. It was so sudden she could hardly catch her balance. The floor seemed to shift under her feet as she walked, and by the time she reached the office door, her face was filmed with perspiration.

"Bev? What's wrong?" Lydia said, standing.

"I don't know." She turned back to them, and the room went pale, then blindingly white. "I think I'm going to faint," she said, sliding to the floor.

"Pregnant? That's impossible!" Bev gaped at the doctor from the emergency room examining table and shook her head. "I can't be pregnant now."

The young resident laughed softly. "Tell that to the baby you're carrying."

Bev just couldn't fathom it. She kept shaking her

head until finally she began to feel dizzy again. "It's impossible. Nothing ever happened before."

"Something happened this time," he said, busily making notes on her chart. "Maybe you've been more relaxed lately, less anxious about getting pregnant."

Bev glanced up at him and nodded, but she hadn't really heard him. "We tried for *five* years."

The doctor met her gaze over his clipboard, smiling this time. "In that case, congratulations."

"Congratulations?" Bev echoed as it finally dawned on her. "I'm pregnant. This is terrible."

"Doctor!" A nurse burst into the room. "There's a man in the hall who insists on seeing the patient. I asked him to wait, but he won't listen."

A man? Bev's heart leaped as the door swung open. For one crazy, ridiculous instant, she thought it might be Sam. She even imagined she saw Sam's face as the man stormed in the room. But as soon as her visitor opened his mouth, Bev knew she'd been hallucinating.

"B.J.!" Harve Brewster bellowed. "Are you okay, baby? What happened? They told me at the office that you fainted."

"I'm okay, Dad," she assured him.

"What do they say it is, B.J.? You been eating right?" He swung around to the doctor. "It's not a brain tumor, is it?"

Bev could see that her father was worried sick. She would have preferred waiting to tell him, but she knew he would drive the hospital staff crazy if she held out. "It's nothing serious, Dad, really. They say I'm . . ." She smiled apologetically as though she was asking permission. "Pregnant?"

"Pregnant?" Harve's face flushed crimson as he stared at her, and then his voice dropped to an incredulous whisper. "You, B.J.? Pregnant? How did that happen?"

"The usual way, I guess."

"You're having a baby?" He clapped a hand to his chest, totally baffled. "I can't believe what I'm hearing! Who's the father?"

"Dad, can we discuss this later?" Bev glanced over at the doctor, who nodded hurriedly, still making notes as he left.

"No, we can't discuss it later," Harve said, storming her bedside. "You're my daughter. I didn't even know you were dating. Who is this guy? Why haven't I met him?"

There was no stopping him now, she realized. She'd created a monster. She would have to tell him or go into hiding. "You have met him, Harve. It's Sam."

"Sam? *My* Sam? You and Sam Nichols?" Harve spun away as though trying to catch his breath, and then he turned back slowly. "He's going to marry you, of course."

"No, Dad, he's definitely *not* going to marry me."

"Why not? I'll—"

"Dad! That's not how it is."

"I'll tell you how it is." Harve balled a fist and slammed it into his open palm. "I never should have saved the miserable bum's life, that's how it is."

Twelve

"Give me a bottle of something," Sam said, pushing his empty beer can across the bar. "Anything but Caribbean rum."

The Red Monkey's bartender rubbed his stubbly jaw. "Maybe you ought to stick with beer, Sam. You've been hitting it pretty hard. Mixing is sure to mess you up."

"That's the point."

"Don't go getting drunk and disorderly on me, okay, buddy? I'd hate to see you do something stupid."

"The bottle." Sam's tone left no doubt about his intentions. If he didn't get the booze, he'd go over the counter and help himself. *Do something stupid?* He nearly choked on that one. His buddy, the bartender, obviously didn't understand. Sam was drinking to *keep* from doing something stupid.

Sam's personal code of ethics wouldn't have won him a round of applause in church on Sunday, but the one thing he didn't do was drink and drive. He'd gotten himself good and wasted every night that week precisely because it kept him *in* the neighborhood bar and *out* of his ragtop convertible. Otherwise he'd be out cruising the lonely streets at night and ending up Lord only knew where.

The last time he'd gone cruising, he'd ended up

parked outside Brewster's waiting to get a glimpse o
B.J. It wasn't the first time he'd found himself there–
and it wouldn't be the last, he knew. The week he'
returned from Nassau, he'd gone nearly nuts with th
need to see her, to set things straight and tell her th
real reason he ran like hell from relationships. It ha
nothing to do with other women. He'd hadn't looked a
a woman since he met her. It was fear. Gut fear. He wa
afraid of that day when his reckless ways would n
longer intrigue her, of that day when she would ask hin
to change, to be some other man . . . *the man sh*
really wanted.

He'd watched her leave Brewster's that night on th
dot of five, wearing her polyester slacks and her lace
collared blouse. And once again he'd told himself t
sober up and smell the coffee. It was business as usua
for B.J. Brewster. She wasn't pining away for San
Nichols's thrill-a-minute lifestyle. She'd made the ad
justment without a hitch.

So be it, he'd told himself all the way back to his rat'
nest of an apartment. So be it. She'd looked happy. Or a
least content. What gave him the right to clear hi
conscience at her expense? He'd given her enough grie

"Hey, Nichols—"

Sam heard the gruff male voice, but he wasn't in an
mood for conversation. "Later," he said as the intrude
began to tap his shoulder.

"I want to talk to you, buddy."

"Give it a rest," Sam warned. Where the hell was th
bartender with that bottle? As a set of beefy fingers du
deep into Sam's shoulder, he swung around, ready to d
damage if he had to. The huge fist came at him so fast
there wasn't time to duck. A haymaker punch caugh
him square on the chin and sent him reeling.

He took a barstool down with him and landed on it
breaking most of the rungs. Pain shot through him
muscles were wrenched under the bruising impact, an
ribs screamed in protest. At least it wasn't his bad side
he thought, grimacing. Now he'd have a matching set c

scars. He shook his head to clear it, rubbed his throbbing jaw and looked up at the guy who decked him. Harve Brewster? "Why'd you do that?"

"This is how you repay me?" Harve bellowed, shaking his fist. "I save your worthless life and all I ask in return is that you keep my daughter out of harm's way—my *only* daughter! And this is how you repay me?"

"What did I do?"

"Don't give me that innocent act," Harve growled, pulling Sam to his feet. "Come on, *son*. We got some talking to do."

Bev was all set to clean Moby Dick's bowl when her doorbell rang. "Who's there?" she called out, coming out of the kitchen with a load of algae cleaner, a pink plastic bucket, and her rubber gloves.

"Delivery for B.J. Brewster."

Delivery? She hadn't ordered anything. "Just a minute," she said, setting her equipment on the floor. She straightened her blouse and tried to sweep flyaway tendrils of hair into her pink bandanna, but the moment she opened the door, her hand stilled and her heart nearly stopped.

She gaped at the whoppingly big bouquet of freshly cut daffodils in front of her. And at the man who held them.

"Sam? What are you doing here?"

"Bringing you flowers?" He held out the bouquet tentatively, as though he weren't at all sure of his welcome.

Bev couldn't have welcomed him if she'd wanted to. She felt as though the floor had dropped out from under her. She stepped back, her stomach lurching as a wave of dizziness washed over her. She was going to be sick! "Excuse me," she cried, signaling him to stay where he was as she made a dash for the bathroom.

"What's wrong?" he called after her.

She didn't actually lose the oatmeal she'd eaten for

breakfast, but it was a close call. Morning sickness! Her only prior brush with it had been some queasiness on arising. She hadn't realized how lucky she'd been. Once her stomach had settled down, she ran a damp cloth over her face and neck, and steeled herself to go out and face him again.

"Are you okay?" he asked as she returned to the living room. He was still standing on the threshold, daffodils at half mast, concern brimming in his blue eyes. She'd been so startled when she opened the door, she hadn't noticed how drastically he'd changed. His trademark aviator sunglasses were resting on the top of his head, tucked into thick dark hair that was neatly swept back off his face. It actually looked as though he'd used a comb instead of his hands. He was clean-shaven, clear-eyed, and smiling without noticeable tension. Only his black leather jacket saved him from being mistaken for a yuppie.

"B.J.? Are you okay?"

"I'm fine," she said quickly. "It must have been something I ate."

He looked as though he wanted to laugh. "I've been told I have a strange effect on women, but I've never had one throw up on me before."

"It's nothing, really. Just a touch of . . ." She checked the phrase on her lips, glancing up at him.

He said it for her. "Morning sickness?"

A highly unladylike word slipped out of Bev's mouth as she stared at him. "You know about the baby?" He knew about the baby. Why wasn't she surprised? "Harve told you, right?" She threw up her hands in exasperation. "Where is he now? Waiting out in the car with a sawed-off shotgun?"

"Harve has nothing to do with the reason I'm here, B.J. I came to see you."

His expression had the grave, handsome cast to it that she had found irresistible during their cruise. Not only that, his baby-blue eyes were imploring her to be reasonable. He was using every weapon in his arsenal, but Bev wasn't in the mood to be won over so easily.

"Can we talk?" he asked.

"Yes, we can talk, Sam," she said quietly. "You're darn right we can talk. And you can start by answering a few questions." She eyed him suspiciously, a trial lawyer cross-examining a reluctant witness. "What are you doing here, looking like that? Clean-shaven? Flowers?"

"What's wrong with the way I look? And since when can't a man bring a woman flowers?"

"Any other man, maybe, but not you. Sam 'The Wild Man' Nichols with a bouquet of daffodils?" She shook her head. "What's next? You're going to propose to me?"

He looked startled, a man caught in the act.

Bev gaped at him. "Oh, no! I don't believe this!" She crossed the room and did an about-face, still incredulous. "You actually have the nerve to come over here, knowing I'm pregnant, knowing I'm carrying your child, and ask me to marry you?"

"Is that bad?"

"It's worse than bad, it's humiliating! You didn't come of your own free will. You're here to do the 'right thing.' What did Harve do? Threaten you with a paternity suit? Or maybe murder by means of castration? That sounds more like Harve."

Sam stepped over the threshold, suddenly very serious. "I'm here because I want to be here, B.J. Get that straight."

Bev took a deep, shaking breath. She'd been secretly thrilled to see him, but she wanted nothing to do with this cowardly act of conscience. "Well, I want you to leave. Get that straight. I'm not marrying a man who feels indebted to my father."

"That debt was paid with the Covington case. I'm here because—" His jaw flexed painfully, and his eyes narrowed to a dazzling slash of light. "Because I love you."

Bev's heart took off like a skyrocket. She folded her arms to hide the explosion of inner trembling. Never in her wildest dreams had she expected to hear such a thing from him. Never. She wanted desperately to believe him, but in her heart of hearts she couldn't. If she'd ever seen a man painfully determined to do his duty, it was Sam Nichols.

She felt weak from shock. Her head was spinning and so was her stomach—again. For one horrible second she thought she really might lose her oatmeal right there in front of him. "I think you'd better go now," she said. "And go quietly. Because I'm not feeling well."

"If you're sick, I should stay."

"If you stay, I will be sick." Bev waved him out the door, and when he refused to budge, she unleashed her ultimate weapon. "I know you don't want to do anything to upset me, Sam," she said firmly, "because that could be bad for the baby."

She had him over a barrel and they both knew it.

He set the daffodils down. "All right, the first round is yours, Slugger," he said, his voice a vibrant whisper. "But don't think the match is over." His gaze drifted to her belly and then he tossed her a wink. "Was that quiet enough for you and Sam, Jr.?"

More daffodils arrived the very next day. A beautiful bouquet greeted her at work in the morning. Another enormous bunch of flowers was waiting for her on her doorstep when she arrived home in the afternoon.

The cards made Bev laugh, and occasionally they made her cry. Sometimes there was a line of poetry by Shelley or Byron that brought tears to her eyes. Sometimes the poetry was less exquisite and more to the point. One card read:

> Roses are red, daffodils are yellow.
> Bev should marry Sam
> because he's a sweet *guy* fellow.

She laughed *and* cried at that one, especially since he'd so plainly proved her wrong about his being a poet.

But the card that broke her heart had one simple line. "I'm sorry." Her chin trembled and tears burned her eyes as she read it. She almost gave in, but something wouldn't let her. It was too much too soon. She was afraid to trust his sudden turnaround, and she wouldn't have a man marrying her out of obligation.

When she didn't respond to the flowers and cards, the custom-made postcards started coming. One had a picture of Sam on the front, getting his gorgeous black hair trimmed, and waving at her from the barber chair. In another, his five o'clock shadow was losing the battle to a straight-edge razor. The note on the back said: "Marry me before I turn into Dudley Doright!"

There was even a picture of him in a freshly cleaned apartment. He stood triumphant in front of a trash can bulging with empties, a raised broom in one fist, a dustpan in the other.

The pressure on Bev increased as the days ticked by. Sam had powerful allies, her father for one. Harve had turned into a crusader for Sam's cause, and he'd recruited the entire agency.

"Well?" Cory would say every morning when Bev arrived. She knew exactly what he meant. He wanted to know if she'd cracked yet. With the whole office listening, she would answer, "I'm very well, thank you," and retreat to her office.

One Saturday morning as she was trying to make room for yet another bouquet of daffodils, Bev received an urgent telegram:

Meet me at my place at seven tonight. If you still feel the same way after we've talked, I'll get out of your life. Sam.

The message included his address.

Her first reaction was panic, and then it dawned on her that the telegram was an ultimatum. She wasn't caving in to his scare tactics! "I'm not going," she said, repeating the words like a mantra even as she was contemplating what she would wear.

She was on his doorstep at seven, feeling very much like a nervous maiden entering fire-breathing-dragon country. He opened the door on the first ring, and Bev knew she must be staring. He looked like a catalog model in his pink knit sweater, khaki jeans, and Top-Siders. She could hardly believe it was Sam.

"Come on in," he said, husky-voiced.

At least that hasn't changed, Bev thought. He still sounded like a roughneck. She declined his offer of a chair, electing to stand between him and the front door as she glanced around his sparsely furnished, surgically clean apartment.

"Bev," he said, imploring her with his powder-blue eyes, "I'm not going to force you into anything, for heaven's sake. Please sit down."

"No thanks. Sitting down is a gateway position where you and I are concerned. It leads to . . . other things."

He laughed, but she could see that he was taking their meeting very seriously. She felt caught in the gaze of his intensely blue eyes, which she knew from past experience was a very dangerous place to be. "What did you want to say to me?" she asked.

"What do I have to do, Bev? How much more do I have to change before you'll believe I'm sincere."

"I never asked you to change, Sam."

"Then what do you want?"

"A man who's honest . . . a man who honestly loves me."

A muscle worked in his jaw as though he were fighting a powerful emotion. "Oh, babe," he said, his voice aching with husky laughter, "I wish you'd told me that before."

"And I wish you'd asked."

Sam Nichols hadn't changed, she realized. The transformation was all for show, just as she'd feared. He'd sent poetry and flowers, but he hadn't even thought to ask her what she wanted when he launched his campaign to win her over. He was still aggressive and headstrong, a man who acted first and thought about consequences later.

"B.J.—" he started, then his focus veered to a point just behind her, and his face went taut. "Don't move," he said, raising his hands slowly.

Bev had no idea what he was doing. "What's going on? If this is some symbolic act of surrender, it won't work."

"It's a symbolic act of cowardice. There's a man behind you with a gun."

Bev felt something cold and hard press between her shoulder blades. She froze as a man's muffled voice whispered, "Do what I say, b-both of you, and nobody gets hurt."

"Don't do anything stupid," Sam warned the intruder. "Take what you want and get out of here."

"Thanks, I will." The man thrust some rope into Bev's hand and pushed her forward. "Tie your boyfriend up, lady."

"Not again," Bev moaned.

A half-hour later, she and Sam were tied up and laying face-to-face on Sam's bed, while the intruder, dressed in black from his ski mask to his shoes, went through Sam's personal effects, hurriedly filling up a knapsack.

"I don't believe this," Bev whispered to Sam. "Why do people keep tying us up?"

"Just lucky, I guess."

"Lucky?" For a victim of armed robbery, Sam struck her as oddly casual. She also didn't like the intimate crush of his body against hers, though that was hardly his fault. "You're not supposed to enjoy this, Sam. You're being robbed."

"You can quit whispering," Sam said. "He's gone."

"So quickly?" Bev craned her neck around, trying to see behind her. As she turned back, something in Sam's expression riveted her to the spot. There was a flare of desire in his eyes that made her throat go dry. He looked like a man on the brink of something wonderful, or terrible. "Why are you looking at me like that?"

"I hope you meant it when you said you wanted honesty, babe. Because I have something to tell you."

"I did mean it . . . I think."

Emotion tugged at the lines of his face, creating hollows and shadows, paring his handsomeness into something dark and gaunt. Bev couldn't take her eyes off him.

"Your dad told me everything," he said. "Why your husband left, what your life has been like since. Don't be angry at him, B.J. It was what I needed to hear, and he knew it. I've been a selfish, self-pitying bastard for a long time now, thinking about nobody but myself."

She shook her head. "Sam, don't—"

"I have to, babe. I have to say this." His eyes flared again, turning incandescently blue. "I thought I was doing you a favor back in Nassau. I told myself to get out of your life, that you deserved better. But the truth was, I was scared. I didn't think anybody could love a holy terror like Sam Nichols. Attraction, maybe. Sex, su But not love."

Pain stung Bev. "I wish you'd stop," she said, swallowing over the blockage in her throat.

"No, I can't, babe. Hear me out, please. As long as I'm on this honesty kick, there's one more thing." His voice broke slightly. "I do love you, so much it's probably going to be the death of me. But I know I'll die without you. I need you. I need this love I feel for you. I want you in my life, that's all. I want our baby."

Bev dragged in a breath, fighting a surge of sweet ache that felt as though it might burst her heart. The raw force of the emotion astonished her. She was shaking inside, coming apart. Tears soaked her face as she looked up at him.

"Oh, Sam . . ." The words stuck up in her throat, then broke free on a soft sob. "I love you too."

He bent to kiss her, and the touch of his lips was like a benediction. It filled her until she glowed with a warmth that promised to heal the hurts and nurture even the deepest, sweetest longings. She strained against the ropes, needing to be free, to put her arms around him.

"You're sure you love me?" he asked, breaking the kiss to search her face. He looked long and deep into her gray eyes. "Very sure?"

"Yes . . . why?"

"Because I've got one last confession on my soul, and it's weighing heavier by the minute."

Bev hesitated, frightened. "What is it?"

"That masked man? That wasn't an armed robber, it was—"

"Arthur," she breathed.

"You knew?"

She shook her head, laughing, still crying. "I had my suspicions. He kept stumbling over his lines, and once he asked me if the ropes were pinching."

"See what I'll do to get you back," Sam said quietly. "See how desperate I am."

There was love in his husky voice, there was tenderness and sincerity. He'd brought her back to life. He'd given her life, and he was exactly the man she needed. She drew in a deep breath. "If the proposal's still good, the answer is yes. With conditions."

"What are they?" He looked wary. "You want me to sell the ragtop? Torch my leather jacket?"

She laughed softly, joyously, and shook her head. She was going to love watching him learn to trust again, to let down his shield and open his heart. But she loved his roughness too, because she knew the rare and tender feelings it protected.

"My conditions are much harder," she told him. "Promise me you'll stop shaving, let your hair grow back, and chew on a toothpick once in a while. I love it when you do that."

THE EDITOR'S CORNER

Come join the celebration next month as LOVESWEPT reaches an important milestone—the publication of LOVESWEPT #500! The journey has been exceptionally rewarding, and we're proud of each book we've brought you along the way. Our commitment to put the LOVESWEPT imprint only on the best romances is unwavering, and we invite you to share with us the trip to LOVESWEPT #1000. One step toward that goal is the lineup of six fabulous reading treasures we have in store for you.

Please give a rousing welcome to Linda Jenkins and her first LOVESWEPT, **TOO FAR TO FALL,** #498. Linda already has five published romances to her credit, and you'll soon see why we're absolutely thrilled to have her. **TOO FAR TO FALL** features one rugged hunk of a hero, but Trent Farraday is just too gorgeous for Miranda Hart's own good. His sexy grin makes her tingle to her toes when he appears at her door to fix a clogged drain. How can a woman who's driven to succeed be tempted by a rogue who believes in taking his time? With outrageous tenderness, Trent breaches Miranda's defenses and makes her taste the fire in his embrace. Don't miss this wonderful romance by one of our New Faces of '91!

In **THE LADY IN RED,** LOVESWEPT #499, Fayrene Preston proves why that color has always symbolized love and passion. Reporter Cassidy Stuart is clad in a slinky red-sequined sheath when she invades Zach Bennett's sanctuary, and the intriguing package ignites his desire. Only his addictive kisses make Cassidy confess that she's investigating the story about his immensely successful toy company being under attack. Zach welcomes the lovely sleuth into his office and as they try to uncover who's determined to betray him, he sets out on a thrilling seduction of Cassidy's guarded heart. As always, Fayrene Preston writes with spellbinding sensuality, and the wonderful combination of mystery and romance makes this book a keeper.

Glenna McReynolds sets the stage for an enchanting and poignant tale with **MOONLIGHT AND SHADOWS,** LOVESWEPT #500. Jack Hudson blames the harvest moon for driving him crazy enough to draw Lila Singer into his arms the night they meet and to kiss her breathless! He has no idea the beautiful young widow has relinquished her dreams of love. Lila knows there could only be this sensual heat between them—they have nothing else in common. Jack has never backed down from a challenge, and convincing Lila to take a chance on more than one special night together is the sweetest dare of all. A beautiful love story that you won't be able to put down.

Guaranteed to heat your blood is **THE SECRET LIFE OF ELIZABETH McCADE,** LOVESWEPT #501 by Peggy Webb. Black Hawk burns with the same restless fever that Elizabeth McCade keeps a secret, and when this legendary Chickasaw leader hides from his enemies in her house, he bewitches her senses and makes her promise to keep him safe. But nothing can protect her from the uncontrollable desire that flares between them. Elizabeth is haunted by painful memories, while Hawk has his own dark shadows to face, and both must overcome fears before they can surrender to ecstasy. Together these two create a blazing inferno of passion that could melt the polar ice caps!

Marvelous talent Laura Taylor joins our fold with the sensational **STARFIRE,** LOVESWEPT #502. With his irresistible looks, business superstar Jake Stratton is every woman's fantasy, but professor Libby Kincaid doesn't want to be his liaison during his visiting lecturer series—even though his casual touch makes her ache with a hunger she can't name. Jake's intrigued by this vulnerable beauty who dresses in shapeless clothes and wears her silky hair in a tight bun. But Libby doesn't want to want any man, and capturing her may be the toughest maneuver of Jake's life. A real winner from another one of our fabulous New Faces of '91!

Finally, from the magical pen of Deborah Smith, we have **HEART OF THE DRAGON,** LOVESWEPT #503. Set in exotic Thailand, this fabulous love story features Kash Santelli—remember him from *The Silver Fox and the Red Hot Dove*? Kash is prepared to frighten Rebecca Brown off, believing she's a greedy schemer out to defraud her half sister, but once he meets her, nothing about the minister's daughter suggests deception. Indeed, her feisty spirit and alluring innocence make him want to possess her. When Rebecca finds herself in the middle of a feud, Kash must help—and Rebecca is stunned by her reckless desire for this powerful, enigmatic man. Riveting, captivating—everything you've come to expect from Deborah Smith . . . and more.

And (as if this weren't enough!) be sure to look for the four spectacular novels coming your way from FANFARE, where you'll find only the best in women's fiction. **REAP THE WIND** by bestselling author Iris Johansen is the thrilling conclusion to the unforgettable Wind Dancer trilogy. **THE SWANSEA DES-TINY** by much-loved Fayrene Preston is the long-awaited prequel to her SwanSea series from LOVESWEPT. Critically acclaimed Virginia Lynn delivers another humorous and exciting Wild West historical in **CUTTER'S WOMAN,** and Pamela Morsi follows the success of her first book with **COURTING MISS HATTIE,** a very touching story of a spinster who finds true love.

What a terrific month of reading in store for you from LOVESWEPT and FANFARE!

With warmest wishes,

Nita Taublib

Nita Taublib
Associate Publisher, LOVESWEPT
Publishing Associate, FANFARE
Bantam Books
666 Fifth Avenue
New York, NY 10103